BLACK BOUNDS

CHARLOTTE BYRD

ABOUT BLACK BOUNDS

I don't belong with her.

Born into darkness, life made me a cynic incapable of love.

But then Ellie waltzed in. Innocent, optimistic, kind.

She's the opposite of what I deserve.

I bought her, but she she stole my heart.

Now my business is going up in flames.

I have only one chance to make it right.

That's where it happens...something I can never take back.

I don't cheat on her. There's no one else.

It's worse than that. Much worse.

Can we survive this?

"Fast-paced, dark, addictive, and compelling" - Amazon Reviewer ★★★★★

"Hot, steamy, and a great storyline." - Christine Reese ★★★★★

"My oh my....Charlotte has made me a fan for life." - JJ, Amazon Reviewer ★★★★★

"The tension and chemistry is at five alarm level." - Sharon, Amazon reviewer ★★★★★

"Hot, sexy, intriguing journey of Elli and Mr. Aiden Black. - Robin Langelier ★★★★★

"Wow. Just wow. Charlotte Byrd leaves me speechless and humble... It definitely kept me on the edge of my seat. Once you pick it up, you won't put it down." - Amazon Review ★★★★★

"Sexy, steamy and captivating!" - Charmaine, Amazon Reviewer ★★★★★

" Intrigue, lust, and great characters...what more could you ask for?!" - Dragonfly Lady ★★★★★

BLACK EDGE SERIES READING ORDER

✓1. Black Edge

2. Black Rules

✓ 3. Black Bounds

✓ 4. Black Contract

5. Black Limit

CHAPTER 1 - AIDEN

*E*llie has my heart and there's nothing I can do about it.

And the worst part?

Or maybe the best part?

I don't even care.

I've never felt this way about anyone before. I was in love before, at least I think I was. But now, looking back, it all feels a little bit like infatuation instead of real love.

I think about Ellie all the time.

I crave her.

I want to be with her all the time.

When she's not around, I want to call her or text her. Honestly, I feel like a child. Whenever we are apart, even for a few hours, my mind goes back to her.

I think about the way she smells, the way she feels, the way she laughs.

Ellie has an intoxicating aroma of home - lavender and sunshine mixed with love.

She feels like a long lost friend who has always been there for me.

And her laughter - it's the best sound in the world.

When I first met her, it was lust at first sight. I have been with a lot of women, but I've never felt that way about them.

Sure, I found many of them sexy and alluring, but something about Ellie made me stop and drop everything and pay attention to just her.

It's like no one else in the world mattered anymore. No one else existed, except for her. And no one else would ever exist again. But as we started to spend more time together, I found myself falling for her.

I'm not just falling for her, no.

I'm falling in love with her.

I am in love with her.

In November, it's already winter in Maine. The cold is nipping at my nose and my fingertips as I walk back from Mr. and Mrs. Warrenhouse's mansion on the water, back to our cottage.

There are lights all around, illuminating my path, and all of a sudden, it looks like the most beautiful place in the world.

The cloud cover above has splintered and the bright full moon is illuminating the dew on the trees. It smells like it's about to snow.

I know, deep inside of my heart, that there's no one else I would rather be here with than Ellie. Without her, I would probably not see any of this beauty around me at all.

I open my mouth and taste the salty air all around me. I can't remember the last time I ever savored a moment like this. When was the last time that I stopped to smell the flowers, as the saying goes?

I've never considered myself to be a particularly sentimental person and paying attention to all this beauty never really occurred to me before.

It's almost as if it only existed in carefully planned shots in movies and photos, but not in real life. And now, walking all alone, toward my beloved, all I see around me is the beauty that life has to offer.

What was I doing before?

How could I have been so blind to all of this around me?

I wonder. Oh, yes, of course.

Work.

I'm a workaholic, I know that.

Work has always been an escape for me.

Whenever things got tough at home and my parents were fighting, or we were about to get evicted, I just retreated into another world - a world where feelings and beauty were stashed in another place altogether.

In this world, computers, numbers, and math dominated the space.

Everything here made sense.

Everything was rational and orderly.

This tendency has made me a success and made me a lot of money.

But it also took a lot away from me. It prevented me from seeing beauty and love, which is all around. It sucked up my days with meetings and algorithms, instead of life.

Looking back, I can't help but feel conflicted about it. Work has always been an escape and one that I relish. I need to work because without it I feel lost.

It's almost like I don't know who I am. And yet, it also feels incredibly good to just put it aside and live in the moment for once.

It's incredibly freeing to live in the moment and to enjoy all the little pleasures that life has to offer.

And this sudden awareness on my part - of this whole other way of existing - it's all thanks to Ellie.

Without her, my eyes would still be closed.

I would spend all of my days in front of the computer and in meetings with colleagues and shareholders.

All I would ever worry about is my stock price and the next project that Owl would be putting out.

CHAPTER 2 - AIDEN

*T*he irony about this whole thing is that it is also thanks to Ellie that things are looking up with Owl.

If she hadn't invited me to Maine with her and insisted on me coming, I would never have met Robert Warrenhouse. I've heard of him, of course.

Who hasn't?

He and his family are some of the biggest investors in New England, which pretty much means that he's one of the biggest investors in the world.

He and his organization have invested in a variety of

companies with a number of different interests, including lumber, sugar, solar, wind, and real estate.

When he first took me to his library for a little chat, I couldn't help but feel a bit intimidated. I wasn't ready to pitch Owl to him, especially at a difficult time like this.

Blake was one of my friends and my earliest investors. I will never forget how much he had done for the company in the beginning.

But at the same time, I will never forget what he has done to Ellie and how spiteful and small-minded he was after I walked in on them on my yacht.

He was embarrassed and ashamed, and instead of apologizing and admitting his mistakes, trying to make some sort of amends, he got angry and spiteful.

He pretended that he'd done nothing wrong. And for that I can never forgive him.

Well, I've always known that Blake was prideful, and I always knew that it would be this silly pride of his that would lead to his downfall.

But I didn't think he would be so petty as to take down Owl with him.

It is one of my greatest mistakes, and regrets, that I allowed him to deal with the majority of the investors in Owl instead of taking on the responsibility myself.

If I hadn't done that, then he wouldn't have had the opportunity to take them all away from me now.

So, as you can imagine, the conversation I had with Mr. Warrenhouse, or rather Robert as he prefers to be called, was rather tense.

I had a lot to explain because Robert follows financial news closely and has a lot of close advisors.

He was well aware of most of what has been going on with Owl.

A lot more than even the financial reporters out there, but of course he didn't know that it all stemmed from what happened between Ellie and Blake back on my yacht.

That part, I kept to myself because that's what Ellie wants. Still, it's not the easiest thing in the world to explain why and how you're bleeding hundreds of thousands of dollars each day and why you lost a billion dollars in valuation within a few weeks.

Looking back on our meeting, I think what made me stand out in Robert's eyes is that I didn't try to sell him a load of shit.

I was completely honest about my falling out with Blake and even mentioned that it was over my current girlfriend, Ellie, whom he met at the party.

I told him exactly what Blake was doing and the mistake I made in putting him in charge of all investor relations with Owl.

I also told him about my plans for Owl and our plans to monetize the company by going into advertising.

I pointed out the similarities that our proposed advertising approach has to the way that all the big companies out there do advertising, including Facebook, Google, and Amazon.

But I also made sure to point out the differences and what makes our approach unique and even better.

Much to my surprise, Robert is very well versed in tech companies and the way we do business.

I had written him off as an old-school investor, who mainly knew how to make money with commodities and financial instruments rather than new tech, but I was all wrong.

Robert knows a lot about my business and even asked me a few really tough questions about valuation, which I struggled to answer appropriately.

That was a bit of a down point in the conversation. I thought I had lost him for sure. But again, Robert surprised me.

At the end, he said that it all sounded good and that he was basically interested in coming on board.

He still needs to have his team of lawyers and accountants take a look at all the relevant numbers, of course, and make sure that they are all lining up.

But otherwise, I can count him in. He plans on making up for all the money that Blake pulled out of the company plus about 30% of what the company lost as a result of all the other investors who left.

I couldn't believe what I was hearing.

Was this a joke?

Was this really happening?

When we shook hands, I felt like I had just let a big boulder the size of New Zealand drop off my shoulders.

Without his investment, the company was going under fast. I have a meeting with the board of directors next week and I was sure that I was going to get fired then.

Everything that has happened over the last few weeks happened because of me and there was nothing I could say or do to make any of it better.

Until Robert decided to invest, of course. And not just invest, invest so heavily that it would basically bring the company back from collapse.

Without Robert's money, the company would cease to exist. He's putting in hundreds of millions of dollars. Of course, nothing is written in stone or put into an iron-clad contract and signed by me and a team of lawyers, but it's something that I never expected in the first place.

There are still lots of things to worry about. Will his accountants approve of his decision?

Will the numbers line up?

Will his lawyers advise him that this is an unwise decision - to invest in what is basically a failing company, which all other investors are running away from?

But I can't worry about those things right now.

Right now, everything is perfect. Right now, the world is my oyster.

I have Ellie and I have Owl.

There is nothing else that I need in the world.

CHAPTER 3 - ELLIE

WHEN THINGS CHANGE

There's a moment in each friendship when something clicks and you can never go back to how things were.

Standing here, with a shawl of twilight wrapped around us, pushing us closer together, I suddenly feel happy for Tom.

At peace.

I'm glad that he is engaged to a woman he loves.

Before I met Aiden, I was like a puppy dog. Foolishly following him around. Hoping that something would happen even though deep down I knew that it wouldn't.

It couldn't.

But right now?

Well, I don't feel anything but friendship.

"You're just so...amazing," Tom says and puts his hand around my shoulder.

I smile at him. It's not very often that people have friends for life, and I hope that Tom will be in my life when I'm seventy or more.

Tom flashes a smile and moves my hair off my neck.

I smile at him and lean my head against his shoulder.

With my eyes closed, I don't see it coming.

Something presses against my lips and it takes me a moment to realize that it's Tom.

My eyes pop open.

My face freezes.

Every muscle on my face freezes, but Tom just laughs.

Then he buries his hands in my hair and presses his lips onto mine again.

This time, I push him away.

Hard.

"What are you doing?"

"I'm not doing anything."

"You just kissed me!"

"It just felt right."

"Well, you better get a better radar because it didn't feel right at all."

"Yes, it does," he insists.

"Are you seriously telling me how I feel, right now?"

"You know what I mean."

"No, I don't," I say.

He laughs and tries to kiss me again. I push him away again.

"I don't want this, Tom. I don't want you."

The words are sharp and to the point. The joking expression on his face vanishes and morphs into something fractured.

For a moment, I feel a tinge of regret, but it quickly passes.

Tom has no right trying to kiss me again when I already made things perfectly clear about how I felt about him.

"So, you and Aiden...you're what, together now?"

"Yes, actually, we are," I say, taking off his jacket and tossing it in his face. "He's my boyfriend. I don't appreciate you kissing me."

"You know what, Ellie?" Tom says, slurring his words a bit.

Was he always this drunk?

How did I not notice this before?

"Why don't you just go fuck yourself then?" he says

"Now, that's classic," I say. "That's what you always say when you can't come up with anything better."

"What do you want me to say?!" Tom screams at the top of his lungs.

His voice is loud and booming and it sends shivers down my spine.

"What do you want, Ellie?!" Tom booms again.

His voice echoes over the treetops and disappears somewhere far over the ocean. Even though there's a party raging inside with some background music, it suddenly occurs to me that someone inside can probably hear him.

"I don't want anything," I say quietly and turn on my heels to leave.

I need to simmer this situation down.

"Where are you going?" Tom follows me.

He jumps in front of me, blocking me from going inside.

I decide to turn around and head down the steps instead. But again, he catches up with me.

"What do *you* want, Tom?" I ask.

"I want you," he says as a matter of fact.

"Well, you can't have me. I'm with someone else. And even if I weren't...we're not good together, Tom."

"How do you know that?"

"Because we fight all the time. We disagree."

"Do you and Aiden not fight? C'mon, if you fight, that's how you know you care."

"No, that's not true. That's bullshit, Tom. Aiden and I disagree, but we don't fight. I don't have to prove anything to him. And he doesn't have to prove anything to me. Besides, it's not about you and Aiden. It's about me. I don't want you, Tom."

The words sound much harsher coming out of my mouth than I really meant for them to sound, but I stand by them. I look straight into Tom's eyes and refuse to look away. I have to get him to get this part. I have to make him understand.

The expression on his face softens a bit. Finally, I think, he's getting it.

"Fuck you, Ellie," he says after a moment.

Okay, maybe not.

"Okay, fine," I say, walking around him and down the path toward our cottage.

"Fuck you, Ellie!" Tom yells after me. I pray that he doesn't follow me and, for the moment, my prayers seem to be answered.

"And you know what else, I hope your book fails. I hope it is the piece of shit that you're afraid it is."

I shake my head when I hear this.

I can't believe that these words are coming out of the mouth of someone I once cared about very deeply.

Of all people out there, only Tom knows how important my writing is to me.

And here he is shitting all over it.

Wow, what a loser. What a pathetic person he has become.

Tom continues to shout as I close the door to the guesthouse behind me.

At the end, I can't make out any of his words anymore, but I know that they're full of bile and hate. And I can't have that around me anymore.

I deserve better.

Still, knowing all that doesn't change how I feel. I sit down on the edge of the bed and bury my head in my hands.

Tears start flowing and there's nothing I can do to stop them.

CHAPTER 4 - ELLIE

WHEN THINGS START TO LOOK UP...

*B*ack at the cottage, I lose track of time.

At first, I plan to only be here for a few minutes, but my eyes refuse to dry. I continue to cry until all of my makeup is smeared and I have big black circles around my eyes.

I don't know exactly why I'm crying so much. I mean I know that Tom was just drunk and probably didn't mean even half the things that he had said to me.

But I also don't care. I'm done coming up with excuses for his bad behavior and for his hurtful words. He sees me only as he wants to see me, not as I really am, and maybe I see him the same way.

Maybe, that's why I was still hanging on to this idea of us that I'd had since college. Maybe it's all an illusion. In any case, I need to accept that Tom is no longer the friend I'd had all those years and that's a difficult thing to lose in the course of a night.

When I finally get a hold of my emotions, I head to the bathroom to take a look at the damage that I've done with all of my tears.

My face is red and splotchy. My eyeliner and mascara are completely smudged all over my eyes all the way to my eyebrow line.

The remnants around my lash line are making their way into my eyes, creating a burning sensation that makes it feel like I have a thousand little tiny razor blades slicing at my corneas. I turn on the water and splash some on my face.

I take a small hand towel, soak it in lukewarm water, and then wipe every bit off my face. When I finally look in the mirror again, I'm no longer such a mess.

Unfortunately, all the crying has left a mark that will probably be difficult to cover up completely, even with a full face of makeup.

Just as I'm deciding what to do next, put on makeup again and return to the party, or just stay here for the rest of the night, Aiden walks through the door. His demeanor is upbeat and he has a wide smile on his beautiful face.

"Hey, babe," he says, giving me a kiss on my forehead. "What's wrong? What happened?"

Everything about his sunny disposition disappears in a second and is quickly replaced by a look of concern and worry.

"No, nothing," I say.

"You look like you've been crying."

Dammit.

I really thought I could just get away with saying that my makeup was bothering me and that's why I had to take it off. Why does he have to be so observant?

I try to play down what happened with Tom by just going over the big points.

"He tried to kiss you?" Aiden asks. "And then he told you to fuck off? What an asshole."

Okay, maybe leaving out most of the details wasn't such a bright idea, I decide.

"Listen, none of that matters, okay? I took care of it. We don't have to make it a thing."

"Of course it's a thing, Ellie. I mean, who does he think he is saying those things to you?"

"I don't know," I say. I walk up closer to him and put my arms around his shoulders. "But it's all over. It's between me and Tom. I don't want you to get into a fight over this or anything else. I don't even want you talking to him."

"I don't know." Aiden shrugs me off, clearly angry.

"Please. I mean, we're here as guests of his fiancée's parents. I don't want this to get worse. Plus, he's really wasted. So, I don't even know if he will remember any of this in the morning."

Aiden shakes his head, pacing around the room.

I feel myself getting through to him because he is a sensible person who isn't one to fly off the handle at a moment's notice.

Aiden isn't a hothead, and that's what I love about him. I know that he cares about me but that doesn't mean that he has to start fights for no reason.

Especially, when there is actually no reason to start one. What happened between Tom and me is between Tom and me.

"You seemed to be in such a good mood when you first walked in." I try to change the subject. "Did you want to tell me something?"

I wait patiently for Aiden to respond and after a few moments, he eventually does. "Actually, yes, I did have some good news."

"Really?" I ask, my eyes light up. I really could use some good news right about now.

"Well, I had that private chat with Robert in his study," Aiden says. "And he seems very interested in investing in Owl."

"Really?" Oh my God, I can't believe it."

"Well, nothing's official yet. But I went over the basics and his eyes definitely didn't glaze over like many other people I've spoken to. He has invested in a few other tech companies and has been on the lookout for a bigger fish for quite some time."

"Oh, wow, that's awesome news, Aiden," I say, wrapping my hands around his neck and giving him a big wet kiss on the lips.

He reciprocates and buries his strong hands in my hair, tugging slightly until I let out a moan.

"But what about all that's been going on with the other investors pulling out? Does he know about that?" I ask in between my kisses.

"Yes, somewhat. I mean, he's pretty up to date on everything they've been covering on the news. I went over the details with him, but he didn't seem phased, which is pretty awesome."

"I know." I kiss him again. He kisses me back and pushes me down onto the bed. We lose ourselves in our bodies for a few minutes until I say, "but what about the party? Shouldn't we go back?"

"Maybe in a bit," Aiden says. "No one is going to miss us."

I don't believe him for a second, but I can't push him away that easily.

I want him.

I need him.

I crave him.

And suddenly, nothing else matters.

CHAPTER 5 - ELLIE

AFTER THE PARTY...

*A*fter Aiden comes to the cottage and tells me all the good news about what Robert said and his interest in investing and saving Owl, we are supposed to go back to the party.

That's why we're here after all.

That's why we came all the way to Maine - to meet all the fabulous people that Tom, Caroline, and her parents, Mr. and Mrs. Warrenhouse, know.

We're at their annual fall party in their sprawling 1890's Queen Anne estate overlooking the vast Atlantic Ocean, and it would be rude not to go back to the party. I know all of these things. Of course, I do.

And yet, when I look into Aiden's fierce eyes and see that mischievous way that he's looking at me at this point, I know that he has other plans. And I know that I won't be able to resist.

"I want you," he whispers.

"I want you, too," I say, but try to get away.

"What do you think you're doing?"

"We can't just stay here. There's the party—"

"Oh, who cares? They won't miss us."

I'm not so sure that's true, but when Aiden wraps his arms around me and licks my ear lobe, I suddenly forget all obligations. I feel his thick cock pushing into my back and I get wet.

"I want you, now," he says. But before he even makes a move, I lunge at him and we collide. Our mouths slide over each other. He lifts me up and wraps my legs around his hips. He carries me, stumbling, to the couch in the corner of the room. Right when we get there, we collapse under our combined weight.

I find myself sprawled underneath him. Suddenly, I'm naked from the bottom down. My dress is around my waist. I try to catch my breath, but he slides to his knees and opens my legs. This time, he isn't slow or deliberate.

He is rushed and impatient. He has to have me right now. He licks me a few times and then shoves his cock inside of me. I get wet immediately and open up for him. He massages my clit as I open my hips wider and wider to welcome him even deeper.

"Aiden!" I moan, digging my fingers into the couch. He pushes my shoulders into the couch and pushes his body away from me. He's holding me perfectly still and having his way with me.

"Ellie." He leans down over me. He covers my mouth with his and our tongues collide. His movements speed up and he burrows himself deeper inside of me with each lunge forward.

"You're mine," he mumbles.

He wants to possess me and the thought of that drives my lust up the wall.

My body quickens and tightens with each thrust.

Suddenly, his body erupts in a loud groan as he comes inside of me.

I hold him close as he climaxes, running my fingers over the protruding muscles in his back.

When he's done, he sighs deeply and pulls out my breast and pops it into his mouth.

He stays in me for some time, licking my nipples. When he does eventually pull out, he only does it to reposition himself.

"What are you doing?" I ask.

"Well, you didn't think we were done yet, did you?" he asks. He lies flat on his back and pushes me on top of him. His cock is not as hard as before, but it quickly grows in strength.

"How are you so hard?" I ask.

"I'm always hard for you."

Aiden cups my breasts and closes his eyes. He starts to move his hips to nudge me and quickly I take over.

"Come for me," he says and that pushes me over the edge.

I start to whimper and moan as the orgasm comes much faster than I ever expected it to.

Much faster than before. It rolls through me like a wave of pleasure.

I clench my thighs and hope I don't fall off.

But he's holding me tight, even as my body goes limp from all the warmth and pleasure that just rushed through every last bit of it.

As I collapse on top of him, time stands still and nothing else exists or matters in this moment but us.

————

AFTER WE MAKE LOVE, I can't sleep.

My mind is going a million miles a minute, and I feel like I just downed a can of energy drink.

I look over at Aiden.

He has the exact opposite reaction to sex.

His arms are wrapped tightly around me, but his eyelids are heavy and droopy.

He can barely register what I'm saying and doesn't really respond.

He's falling asleep.

Fast.

I don't mind.

I give him a brief peck on the forehead and extricate myself from him.

I push his arms back to himself and pull the covers tightly around him.

He's so beautiful when he sleeps; it actually causes me pain to look at him. But a good kind of pain.

Since it already feels like it's the middle of winter outside, I get dressed as soon as I get up and wrap myself tightly in a scarf that I brought for the occasion.

Despite the cold, my body feels so antsy that I consider going outside.

But I don't want to put on a coat and boots just quite yet.

Instead, I do a few stretches and yoga moves to calm myself down.

Reaching up to the sky and around for three sun salutations, I immediately feel a little bit more at ease.

I close my eyes with each deep, deliberate breath, and when I open them again, they focus on one thing on the far side of the room.

My laptop.

My fingers almost ache to open it.

No, I shouldn't do it, right?

I should just get back into bed, snuggle up to Aiden, and try to sleep.

But when I look back at him and how comfortable and gorgeous he looks sleeping, I know that I won't be able to fall asleep.

Not yet.

No, what I really want to do right now is write. What's wrong with that? I mean, why can't I?

Deciding not to fight my urges anymore, I sit down at the desk and open my laptop.

Typically, if I'm procrastinating and wasting time, I first check my emails.

Then I read some news. Then I take some quizzes on

BuzzPost. Then I read some useless celebrity gossip on sites like *Daily Mail* and *US Weekly*.

But tonight is different.

None of those things interest me much at all.

No, instead, all I want to do is open the last thing I've written for *Auctioned Off* and continue the story of us.

It's as if I need to get it down to make sure that I don't forget anything. It's as if it has to be written to make it real.

When my writing is going well, there's a flow to it. There's nothing more natural and easy. I simply put my hand to the keyboard and words just come out.

Sometimes, I can't type fast enough to actually catch up with what I'm trying to say.

The world outside stops existing and I lose all sense of time and place. The words and the characters on the page are the only things that exist.

I don't even stop long enough to wonder if I exist. I know I don't.

Instead, I'm simply a vessel for the muse. I am the

physical being writing down what is going on out there between the two of them.

The reality between fiction and real life blurs so much that when my characters suffer, I suffer.

When they are happy, I am happy.

When they cry, I cry.

When my writing is going well, it becomes so much more meaningful than what's going on out here.

Except that this story is different, of course.

This story isn't fiction.

It's the truth.

It's what really happened between Aiden and me. Here, I'm not making anything up.

What I experienced is exactly what's in the story. And that makes the writing even more meaningful, in a way.

I can live through those moments I cherished and those moments that terrified me again and again.

As I write, I don't really know where I'm headed with this book. I don't have an outline or a plan.

Instead, I simply sit at the keyboard and bleed onto the page. I'm using fake names, but the characters are us. And will always be us.

Suddenly, a strong pang of fear hits me. I tense up for a moment and consider the question.

Will I be strong enough to write the truth even when it's not something pleasant anymore?

I mean, the way that Aiden and I met was exciting and enticing. But what about what happened with Blake?

Will I be able to write the truth about what he did to me?

And what he's now doing to Owl?

I'm still a bit off from there, but those moments are coming. Especially, if I intend to write the whole truth as it happened. Is a pseudonym enough of a protection to tell the truth and keep what is private between us?

I don't know the answers to these questions. The more I think about that, the more questions I come up with, without many accompanying answers.

Eventually, I decide to put these feelings aside and focus on the task at hand.

I write for almost two solid hours and my hands ache when I stop. I have been typing too fast and for too long. I rub my wrists to relieve some of the pressure as I scroll through the pages that I've written. The words aren't perfect, of course.

It's just the first draft.

But it's a rather good one. I change very little except for punctuation and typos. The words have come out just as they had existed as thoughts in my head.

If you aren't a writer, you might not know, but that's quite a rare thing. Most of the time, you just have a vague idea of where you are headed, but no real way of getting there.

I smile as I save the document on my computer. I'm proud of it because I know it's perfect for what it is - the first draft of the story.

The story isn't complete, nowhere close to it, but it's perfect as what it is.

CHAPTER 6 - ELLIE

I close the laptop and stretch my arms around and behind me. My back cracks as I move my head from side to side.

Wow.

I'm pretty sore.

I have been stuck in a stationary position for quite a while and all the joints in my body feel like they need extra fluids to lubricate them. I haven't worked this hard and focused this intensely for what seems like forever. Even my face feels tense. I rub my temples and stretch out every limb in my body. I feel excitement pulsing through my veins. When I glance at myself in the mirror, I see a wide, broad smile stretching across my whole face. I'm even smiling with my eyes.

I peek outside, past the blinds and the curtains. The sun is barely up. Only the idea of morning exists as a sliver of yellow somewhere over the horizon. A part of me wants to rush over to Aiden, wake him up, and tell him about everything that I have just accomplished. I can't just keep this to myself. I feel like it's bursting out of me. But when I glance over at him, I see how peaceful he's sleeping, even snoring a little bit every third breath, and I don't have the heart to wake him up. No, this can wait. He needs his rest. All the emotional upheaval over Owl, and Robert Warrenhouse coming in last minute and saving the company from total collapse must have taken a toll on him. All the stress and lines around his face have straightened out. All the tension that has been sitting somewhere between his eyebrows has dissipated.

I pace around the room trying to think of something to do. I thought that writing would put my mind at ease and calm me down, but I'm still riding a high. I feel like I drank four cups of coffee, even though I haven't had any caffeine since yesterday morning.

So, I decide to take a walk. I see little white flurries hit against the windows and decide that I definitely need boots and a coat. A hat and a scarf will also not hurt anyone. I've always been quite a wimp when it comes to the cold. I don't know if it's my body temperature being naturally cooler than other people's, or my slow metabolism, but I'm always cold. Even in the summer. I always need at least two more layers than other people just to stay warm, and running in place or doing some exercises doesn't help much. I just get sweaty and then I'm even colder than before.

I slip my feet into a thick pair of my favorite Uggs and relish how comfortable they feel. They aren't the most attractive boots, but they are perfect for an early morning walk around the property. Then I put on a thin, long-sleeved sweater and wrap my favorite pale pink scarf around my neck. After I put on a hat and my jacket, I'm ready to brave the cold. But before I step outside, I run over to the computer again. In all the excitement, I had completely forgotten to check on my sales and book downloads. I'm not expecting much, but every sale is a small victory. I'm still in shock that anyone is interested in the story that I have to tell, let alone are paying me to tell it.

When the Amazon dashboard finally loads, I almost scream out in excitement. Fifty three sales! Oh my God! No, this can't be right. I reload the page, but there it is. The sales are legit and now there are fifty four sales. In addition, I also have five thousand page reads! I shake my head, unwilling to believe my own eyes. Is this really happening? I mean, am I really making money being a writer? Is this what it feels like to live your dream?

I can't contain my excitement much longer and decide to step outside before I wake up Aiden. When I get out to the porch, I let the burst of cold air wash over me. I inhale deeply and savor the smell of the salt water. The ocean is less than a hundred feet away and I stand on the steps of the cottage, watching its slow and mesmerizing waves crash against the beach. Finally, my anxiety and excitement is starting to subside. I'm still riding a high, but the sight of water has always had a calming effect on me.

I walk down the path and toward the main house. I don't have a destination in mind; it just feels good to walk. Most of the cars that were parked out front are gone, along with the valet people. There are some party favors and empty cans and cups scattered out on the front lawn. Wow, people can be very disrespectful. The Warrenhouses put on this awesome party that must've cost them a fortune, and the guests still don't bother to clean up after themselves. Even in the mildest, smallest way. I toss all the trash that I pick up into the empty garbage pails near the porch. I consider heading into the house, but don't want to disturb anyone just in case they are sleeping already.

A strong gust of wind rushes through me and I zip the jacket tighter to keep some of the cold out. I bury my hands in my pockets and find my phone. Oh, yes, of course! I completely forgot about it. I won't lie. I'm kind of a phone addict. I'm usually on my phone most of the day. If I'm not talking on it, I'm texting or checking my emails, or wasting time on Facebook and Instagram. But somehow, I have completely forgotten about it for close to twelve hours. Very impressive, Ellie, I say to myself.

But as soon as I look at the screen, my pride vanishes immediately. I have four missed calls from Caroline and another ten texts. Shit, I say to myself. I scroll through her texts and listen to her messages. Caroline isn't big on leaving voice mails, so I know that this is important.

What could she want? I wonder. Her first texts came in around one in the morning and the rest came soon after. Then suddenly, nothing. Crickets. Maybe she wanted a ride home. Maybe something happened with her date? What was his name? My mind is running in circles. She came here with the guy she met at the auction on Aiden's yacht. She has seen him a number of times before, and he has even been to our house. But that doesn't mean that he's completely trustworthy, does it? I mean, what do we really know about him except that he has a lot of money and is willing to spend almost a hundred grand for a one night stand? I can't remember exactly how much Caroline got, but it was enough to pique her interest. Besides, she wasn't really supposed to see him after the auction, but he made an impression. He asked her out once they were both back in the city. He was genuinely interested in her. At least, it seemed that way.

CHAPTER 7 - ELLIE

WHEN I TRY TO FIND CAROLINE...

I walk around the property, feverishly texting her. I don't bother to wait for her to answer and call her as well. But no one responds. The call goes directly to voice mail and the text goes unread. Caroline is never without her phone. This isn't good, I say to myself. But then I realize that there may be a perfectly reasonable explanation for her not answering as well. I mean, I'm as much of a phone addict as she is and my phone was just in my jacket while I was busy with Aiden. And then, of course, there's sleep. She always turns her phone to 'Do Not Disturb' once she goes to bed. Otherwise, she wouldn't get a wink of sleep. All the notifications would drive her completely nuts.

Meandering through the meticulously manicured
foot paths around the back of the Warrenhouse
mansion, I come up on one cottage upon another.
The one that Aiden and I are staying in is just one of
the many guesthouses that exist on the property.
Caroline must be staying in one of these. But, which
one? Each one has a little white picket fence out
front with rose bushes. The sun is just starting to
peek over the horizon, making the space out here
look like an enchanted forest. The Warrenhouses
must spend a fortune on gardeners to make
everything look so shabby chic. The plants, bushes,
and trees are just overgrown enough to give the
illusion of a quaint English garden. It's perfect, but
not too perfect. If I weren't so focused on finding out
if Caroline is okay, I would love to lose myself in
this world.

Meandering past the guesthouses, I notice that there
are cars parked out back, just outside the main
garden areas. They are tucked out of sight and out of
mind, as if they are keeping the twenty-first century
at bay. I try to remember which car Caroline took to
get here. I'm pretty sure that her date rented a car,
but what kind? I walk past a Bentley, a brand new

Tesla, and a couple of other name brand cars that I know cost a fortune but not exactly how much.

Once I reach the edge of the guesthouses, I shrug and turn around. I feel like crying because I'm at a complete loss as to how to go about finding Caroline. Or whether I even should. I mean, it's barely morning and the last thing I want to do is barge in on her sleeping and create a scene. Or even worse - what if I were to barge in on a couple of complete strangers? No, I guess I should just make my way back to Aiden and just wait until it's a more reasonable hour before finding her.

I take a deep breath and try to calm myself down. Just because she called you earlier, doesn't mean anything. I mean, she didn't come around looking for you. Everything is probably fine. I mean, when is it not? I know that bad things happen out there, but that doesn't mean that they're going to happen here in this multimillion dollar mansion overlooking the Atlantic Ocean. I'm just overthinking things. I'm riding a high from having one of the best orgasms of my life, and then seeing that all those people have downloaded my book, and having an awesome writing session. That's why I can't quiet my mind down. It has nothing to do with Caroline. Yes, of course.

I'm not always successful in talking myself down, but this morning I surprise myself. In addition to calming my erratic thoughts with soothing thoughts, I also do a breathing exercise that I learned in yoga class. I close one nostril and take a big breath in. Then I open it, pinch my other nostril and breathe out through the other one. This focuses my breathing and I feel myself taking in air further into my stomach instead of just into my lungs. Okay, okay, I say to myself. Everything's going to be fine. There's nothing to worry about. Just go back to Aiden and try to get some sleep.

I make my way down the now familiar path back to our cottage at the very end. But just as I walk past the one with the bright blue door, I hear a familiar voice. I can't make out what he's saying. It sounds more like grunting. Moaning, maybe. I furrow my brows and stop in my tracks. What could that be? I walk over to the window on my tiptoes to take a peek inside. I don't want to draw unnecessary attention to myself just in case the people inside are having a good time.

Luckily, the blinds and the curtains are wide open. I stand really close to the glass and cover my face to block out some of the gray light coming from the outside. Oh my God, I whisper to myself when I see the guy's back to me. He's stark naked except for a pair of black socks and he's having sex with someone who is lying on the bed. I can't see his face or the woman's face, but I can tell that it's a woman because she's still wearing her high heels and her legs are listlessly open to either side of him.

The guy looks familiar, but with him facing away from me, I can't really place him. He must be someone I met at the party since he's staying at a cottage on the Warrenhouse property, but who he is exactly I don't know. Still, I get the sense that I know him. I look at his dark hair and his shoulders. He's relatively thin but muscular as well. Strong.

I watch, feeling very much like the creep that I am. But something is holding me by the window. And it's not anything good. There's something about the girl that doesn't look right. Her legs are spread open before him. He's holding one of them up by his shoulders and the other one is laying bent to the side. But it's the way it's bent. As he continues to come in and out of her, she's barely responding. No, she isn't responding at all. Something feels very wrong about this.

Suddenly, the guy tilts his head back and gives out a big moan. Then he speeds up his tempo. And yet the girl continues to lie there, without much of a response. I glare over to the other side of the door. There's another window there. Maybe it will give me a better angle on what's going on.

Not wanting to look away, but having the urge to get to the bottom of this situation, and to find out if the girl is actually okay, I push myself off the window sill and walk over to the other window. The blinds are down on this one, but they aren't entirely shut. Again, I cover my face and peer in.

My heart drops. At first, I don't believe what I see. This can't be him. No. Can it? I look closer. I can see his profile. No, I'm not wrong. It's Tom.

CHAPTER 8 - ELLIE

WHEN I FIND OUT WHO IT IS...

*a*nd the girl? It doesn't look like Carrie. No, not at all. She's shorter and her face. I can't quite make out her face but that body is not Carrie's. I take a deep breath and look closer. Tom's body is not blocking her from view entirely as before. Now, it's perfectly clear that she is completely passed out. Her body is limp. Unresponsive.

No, no, no. Whoever this is, she looks dead. Or at least, asleep. I have no idea who she is, but one thing is for sure. She's definitely not giving her consent.

Before I even realize what I'm doing, I hop over to the front door and turn the handle. It swings right open. Tom doesn't notice me at first. He continues to make those sickening sounds of pleasure and pump away, holding the girl's legs in the air.

Suddenly, I start to have doubts. What if she is consenting? I mean, I consented to being tied up. Maybe if someone had spied on me and Aiden through the window, they would also think that he was abusing me. But it's too late for any of those thoughts now. I'm here, standing in the doorway. And I have to find out what's happening.

"What are you doing?" I ask loudly. Tom stops in mid-action and turns his head to look at me. Once he sees me, he drops the girl's legs and pulls out. A part of me expects the girl to sit up on her elbows and tell me to get the fuck out, but she doesn't. Instead, what I see is the grave expression on Tom's face. He looks terrified. His eyes shift from side to side, trying to figure out what to say and do.

"Tom, what the fuck?" I ask. No, my initial response to this was correct. Something is off here. I step inside the cottage and walk over closer to the bed. That's when it hits me. The girl on the bed is completely passed out. Unresponsive. Tom grabs his pants and starts to get dressed haphazardly. He puts one foot into the pants, hops around, and almost slips.

Suddenly, everything starts to move in slow motion. I walk over to the girl and my ears start to buzz. Is this really her? My heart starts to beat so fast it feels like it's going to jump out of my chest. I try to inhale, but my chest seizes up.

"What are you doing?" I ask over and over as I drape myself over the girl on the bed. No, it can't be her. It just can't. She's completely nude from the top down, and her dress is pushed up to her waist. I grab her by the shoulders and start to shake her as fast as I can.

"Caroline, Caroline. Wake up, Caroline!"

"She just fell asleep," Tom says somewhere behind me. "She was totally into it before."

I hear him talking, but I'm not entirely processing everything that he's saying. My only focus now is to wake her up. She has to be okay. I have to make her okay.

But no matter how much I shake her, she doesn't respond. No, no, no. Hot tears are streaming out of my eyes. I can't see anything more than a few inches in front of my face.

"Wake up, Caroline," I say over and over. A few of my tears run into my mouth and I choke on them. I cough and wipe my eyes.

I take a deep breath and try to figure out what to do. Then I reach for her neck. I press my fingers to her artery. Please, please, please. Please, let there be a heartbeat. And then I feel it. It's faint, but it's there. Oh my God. Okay, okay, I say to myself. I kneel down and press my head to her lips. Please, breathe on me, Caroline, I say to myself silently as I wait.

Somewhere behind me, Tom is saying something. He's rushing around the room. He's freaking out, but I can't pay attention to him at all. It's almost like nothing else exists except for this moment right now. And then, suddenly, she breathes. I clearly feel her breathe in and out, and I exhale deeply myself. Okay, at least she's alive. Despite anything else that happened.

Still, she's unresponsive. So, I need to act fast. I bury my hands in my jacket and pull out my phone. My hands are shaking so violently, I can barely make out the numbers. Luckily, there are only three. 911.

"What's your emergency?" a woman asks on the other end.

"What are you doing?" Tom asks, grabbing the phone out of my hand. I stare at him.

"Give me that phone. Caroline is passed out!" I yell loudly. He hasn't hung up yet and I need to get the message out to the 911 dispatcher.

"No, she's just sleeping."

"You were having sex with her. She's completely unresponsive. And you were having sex with her, Tom. Give me that phone."

"No," he says and hangs up. Then he puts my phone in his pocket and glares at me. Shit. Cold sweat courses through my veins. It suddenly occurs to me exactly the kind of vulnerable situation that I'm in. I'm alone in this room with him. Caroline is passed out. I had just caught him doing something to her that he has no right to. And he has taken away my phone. He's growing desperate and desperation is never a good quality in men. That's when violence comes about.

"What are you doing, Ellie? You're going to call the cops on me? I'm your friend."

"I know that," I say slowly. "You are. But we need to get her help. I don't know why she's not responding, Tom. Maybe she had too much to drink. But I think she needs medical help. That's the whole reason I was calling them."

Tom paces around the room. I glance at the door at the far corner. That's my way out, but he's standing in front of it. I can try to run for it, but what if he were to catch me? No, I need to play this smart.

"No, it wasn't," Tom says with a disappointed look on his face. "You were calling to turn me in. But the thing is, Ellie, that I didn't do anything wrong."

"You didn't?"

"No, we were just having sex. And she passed out. But before she did, she was totally into it."

"But what about Carrie?" I ask.

He shakes his head. "I don't know, Ellie. Caroline

was just sitting on the porch. She had a fight with that guy who she came with. We kissed and one thing led to another. You know how it is."

"Yes, of course," I lie. I have to agree with what he says now. That's my only way out. Who knows what he will do to me if I don't pretend to be his friend again. Who knows what he's capable of. I never thought that he would be capable of raping a girl, let alone our friend. But, apparently, I don't know Tom as well as I thought I did. Maybe I never really knew him.

CHAPTER 9 - ELLIE

WHEN I FIND MYSELF IN A TRAP…

"*L*isten, Tom, you have to believe me. I'm on your side. If what you say is true, then let's call the paramedics and get her some help. I mean, this isn't normal. Caroline is our friend."

I'm trying to appeal to his better self. I have no idea if it's going to work. But I'm all out of options.

"No, we can't," he says. He sits down on the couch by the window on the far end of the room, burying his head in his hands. "I really messed up, Ellie. I'm so sorry."

"It's all going to be okay, Tom. I'm here for you."

I debate whether I should come over there and

comfort him. That would make him believe me more, but I'm also terrified of being that close to him. But it may be my only way out. I keep eyeing the front door, hoping that someone, anyone, will just walk in. But it's too early. The world is still asleep. Besides, this is a private cottage and now that he has my phone, I'm totally on my own.

"You're just going to tell them what you saw. But you have to believe me, that's not what happened. I wasn't raping her, or whatever you think I was doing. She was into it. It's not my fault she fell asleep."

"I know that, Tom. And that's what you're going to explain to them. But for now, I just really think we need to have someone check in on her and see if she's okay. She's barely breathing, Tom. Her pulse is very shallow. She needs our help."

He shakes his head.

I take a few steps toward the door, still debating whether I should come over closer to him to make my point stronger or just make a run for it.

"You don't want to make this any worse, do you? I mean, what if she's not okay? And we didn't get her any medical help?"

"No, I can't," he says slowly.

I take a few more steps closer to the door and my freedom.

"Why?"

"Because then Carrie will find out. And I can't have her finding this out, Ellie."

"No, she won't," I say, even though I'm fully aware of how unconvincing I sound. Of course, Carrie will find out. I don't know how she wouldn't. I take another few steps toward the door. I decide to make a run for it when I get a little bit closer. Tom is in such distress that I can't trust any of his reactions. I have no idea what he's capable of and I don't want to find out.

"I'm really, really sorry, Ellie," Tom says. He looks up at me. His eyes are bloodshot and full of tears. His face is red and splotchy. Whatever happened here, he's definitely regretting it. I take a deep breath.

"I know you are," I say. When he hangs his head back down, burying it in his knees, I decide to make a run for it.

Within a few steps, I grab the door handle and turn.

A gust of cold air hits me like a ton of bricks. I'm outside! Yes!

But then someone grabs me by my hair and tugs really hard. My neck throbs from the pain and my whole scalp burns. A primal scream escapes my lips, sending shivers through my whole body.

"Let me go!" I scream at the top of my lungs. Now that I'm outside, making as much noise as possible is my only way out of this. I need someone to come help and for help to arrive, I need attention.

"Tom, no! Let me go! Help!" I yell.

"Shut up! Shut up!" Tom wraps his cold fingers around my throat and mouth. He closes my nose and I struggle to breathe. He's behind me and on top of me. He's smothering me. But I won't go down this easily. No, I'm going to fight.

I elbow him as hard as I can in the ribs. He winces in pain and lets go of his grip on me. I inhale deeply and suddenly, I'm able to breathe in and out again. I scramble up to my feet and head toward the white picket fence. I just need to get to the other side of that, I say to myself. Then I'll be okay.

But he grabs me by my feet before I get there. Both of my feet are suddenly locked in place and I tumble to the ground, bracing my fall with my hands. Once I hit the ground, I make a loud thump and all the wind gets knocked out of me. I struggle to inhale even a tiny bit of air. It takes all of my energy to just flip over on my back so that I can get some more air. Slowly, my airways start to open, but each breath is still the most painful thing that I've ever experienced.

When I'm finally able to breathe somewhat normally, someone climbs on top of me. It's Tom, but I've never seen him look like that before. He's blocking out all of the morning light with his body and he's pinning my hands back behind my head. He's sitting across my torso and I'm unable to move at all.

"What the fuck are you doing, Ellie?" he asks, huffing and puffing through each word.

I have no idea how to answer that question. I just look around and try to figure out what to do next. There has to be a way out of this, right? This can't be it?

He leans over to me and presses his lips to mine. It takes me a moment to realize that he's kissing me. Actually, forcing his tongue down my throat. But I also feel the shift in his weight on top of me. He's no longer pinning my legs down and suddenly they are free. I lift up my leg and kick him as hard as I can in his back. He cries out in pain. But I'm not done yet. I lift up my head and grab a hold of his lower lip, biting down on it as hard as I can. Something wet and warm runs down the back of my throat. He screams out in pain, but I don't let go until I'm ready. Then I push him away from me. He falls on his back next to me, and I see a rock laying next to me. I grab it and hit him as hard as I can in the face. Then I scramble up to my feet and wobble toward the white picket fence and as far away from him as possible.

As soon as I'm outside the fence, I run for it. I don't bother to turn around. I don't bother to see if he's alright. Or even if he's after me. No, I just need to get myself as far away from here as possible and the only way to do that is to run. Run for my life.

I burst through the door of our cottage and lock the door behind me. Aiden lazily opens his eyes.

"What's wrong?" he asks with a perplexed look on

his face.

My heart is pounding so hard, it's practically jumping out of my chest. I try to calm down my breathing, but it's all to no avail. I gasp for breath instead. Aiden gets out of bed and walks over to me. He's still in the nude. I wouldn't be surprised if he had been asleep this whole time. He probably barely moved at all.

"What's wrong, Ellie?" he asks.

I continue to gasp for breath. But in between my quick, dissatisfying breaths, I manage to mumble, "We have to call the police. Can I have your phone?"

Without another question, he runs over to the nightstand and hands me his phone. I dial 911.

"What's your emergency?"

"I tried to call you earlier, but he took my phone away. You need to come right away. I walked in on him raping my friend," I say as calmly as possible.

The 911 operator asks me a dozen other questions, which I answer truthfully and to the best of my ability. I don't keep anything back. I tell her how he took my phone and attacked me. I tell her how I hit him in the head with a rock to get away. I tell her that I have no idea if he's still conscious or if he's even still here. When she asks me where we are located, I turn to Aiden, who tells me the address.

The 911 operator refuses to let me hang up until the police arrive. But I'm too afraid to go outside to see what's going on and when Aiden volunteers to go, I grab his hand.

"But what about Caroline?" he asks. "Don't you want me to check on her?"

"Yes, of course. But she was passed out. What are you going to do for her if you find her that way? We need the paramedics to come here and fast."

"Ellie, I'm just going to check on her."

I shake my head, refusing to let him go. But he pries my hands off him and gives me a big warm kiss on the lips.

"I'm going to be okay; he's not going to do anything to me, Ellie. I promise," Aiden says. In a flash, he pulls on a pair of pants, a long sleeved shirt, his dress shoes, and his jacket from last night. And just like that, he's gone.

CHAPTER 10 - ELLIE

THE AFTERMATH...

I know it's not right that I didn't want Aiden to go help Caroline. I know that he should go. Of course, he should. But I can't help how I feel. I'm afraid. I don't want anything else bad to happen and, at this point, I don't know what Tom is capable of. Still, Aiden doesn't listen to me. He leaves me alone in the room with the 911 operator on the line. I pace around the room, trying to decide what to do. Should I follow after him, just in case he needs my help? Or should I just say here? Stay safe.

The 911 operator keeps asking me questions about what happened and I answer the best I can. I tell her about getting a number of calls from Caroline, and that I didn't see them until later this morning. After a while, we end up covering the same ground. I don't know why I have to stay on the line, but she insists that we should until the police arrive. After what feels like forever, but is probably only ten or fifteen minutes later, I hear sirens somewhere in the distance.

"They're here," I say.

"Okay, just walk out there and make sure that it's them," she says.

I run out of the cottage and see two police cars pulling into the parking lot up front. The paramedics aren't far behind. Aiden meets us out front as well.

"I couldn't find him anywhere," he says with a disappointed look on his face. "But you have to help Caroline. She's still unresponsive."

"Is she breathing?" one of the police officers asks.

"Yes, but very faintly," he says.

The next hour or so is a complete blur. There are so many emergency personnel walking around all over the place that I get overwhelmed and just find a quiet place to sit and wait until someone talks to me.

I watch as the paramedics rush Caroline, on a stretcher, to an ambulance. There are all sorts of tubes attached to her and my eyes well up with tears at the sight.

"At least, she's not coming out in a black body bag," Aiden says. This statement is supposed to make me feel better, but instead, it just makes me feel like total shit. I should've answered her calls and texts earlier. I shouldn't have spent all night making love and then writing. Then maybe none of this would've ever happened.

"She called me. A lot," I say, burying my head in his shoulder. "I should've been there for her."

"This isn't your fault. Not at all," Aiden says. "You had no idea any of this would happen."

I believe him, of course, but only partly. A big part of me doesn't believe him at all. I know what I should've and shouldn't have done, and I know that I had failed her. Even if I didn't know, that's still no excuse.

A police officer approaches us and asks to take my statement. His partner takes Aiden aside, probably to get his own statement.

"Can you tell me what happened?" he asks. I had already told the story to the 911 operator and to Aiden, but I repeat it again. I've seen enough crime shows and true crime documentaries on television to know how this works. They keep asking you to re-tell your story in order to see if you mess up. Or add anything that you haven't added before. It's all about being consistent. It's supposed to point out who the liar is. But I have nothing to hide. I tell him the whole truth and nothing but the truth, exactly how it happened.

The police officer listens carefully and writes down parts in his little notebook.

"Have you found Tom?" I ask at the end.

"Actually, no." He shakes his head. "We can't find him anywhere."

My heart sinks into my stomach. What is he talking about?

"But when he attacked me, I hit him on the head with a rock and he fell down right there. In the front yard," I say.

"And your boyfriend, Aiden Black? Is that his name?" he asks, reading off his notes.

"Uh-huh." I nod.

"He went out to check on Caroline after you ran back to your cottage?" the police officer asks.

"Yes, while I was on the phone with the 911 operator."

"Well, that's the odd thing; he didn't see him either."

I already know this. But I don't really have an explanation as to why not.

"I don't really know what to say." I shrug. "I mean, I hit him hard but it's not like he was dead or anything. Maybe he just ran away. Because he knew I was going to call the police."

"Maybe," the cop says unconvincingly. Suddenly, it hits me. Wait a second. What is going on here? Is he really questioning my story? What does all this skepticism on his face mean? Is he trying to say that I'm lying?

"I don't understand," I say. "Are you trying to imply that you don't believe me?"

Now I feel myself getting angry. I mean, who the hell does he think he is?

"No, not at all. I'm just telling you what we know now."

"Well, I'm not lying. He was the one who did it. He was right there when I left him. If he ran afterward, well, I don't know what I can do about that."

My voice is rushed and on the verge of losing control. I'm angry that he's questioning me after all that I've been through. What gives him the right?

"Okay, I didn't mean to upset you, Ms. Rhodes," the cop says after a moment. "Let me talk to my partner and I'll be right back with you."

He leaves me sitting on the stoop of my cottage. Even though morning is in full bloom already, the air feels colder than it ever did before. Whatever sun peeks through the cloud cover, it's not enough to warm me up. Suddenly, I feel an overwhelming feeling of despair and loss come over me. I want to scream and cry at the same time. I want them to believe me and leave me alone. I want to go back to bed and pretend that none of this ever happened. I want to turn back time. Shivers run through my body and I don't know if they can be attributed entirely to the cold, or the fact that I didn't really sleep at all last night or everything that has happened. Perhaps, it's some sort of combination of all three.

I wrap my arms around my shoulders and rock from side to side. This soothes me somewhat and my heartbeat slows down to its normal pace after a while. I inhale and exhale deeply and force all the bad thoughts swirling around in my head to go away at least for a few minutes.

CHAPTER 11 - ELLIE

"Hey," Aiden says, walking up to me. He's holding two small plastic cups in front of him. I watch the way the steam rises from the top, guided slightly by the breeze off the ocean. Right now, it looks like the most beautiful thing in the world.

"I got us some coffee," Aiden says, handing me one of the cups. I take it and wrap my hands around its hot base. I take a sip and savor the moment of how it runs down the back of my throat.

"This is good," I whisper.

"Yes, it is," Aiden says, wrapping his arm around my shoulders and squeezing me tightly. "Are you okay?"

I give him a little smile, but we both know that it's a lie, that's how utterly unconvincing it is.

"You're going to be okay," he says.

"What about Caroline?"

Aiden shakes his head. "I don't know for sure. But I think she'll be alright, too. She had a pulse and she was breathing."

"Faintly," I correct him. "Barely breathing."

Aiden hangs his head and avoids eye contact with me. He knows that what I'm saying is the truth, and no matter how he sugarcoats it, he can't change that fact.

Neither of us say anything for a while. I look out past the police vehicles and all the commotion to the water on the horizon. The waves are peaceful this morning, not crashing very hard against the sand. It's almost as if they are sad as well.

"Do you want to go inside?" Aiden asks. "It's freezing out here."

I don't respond. On one hand, I wouldn't mind going inside. I'm so cold that I have barely any feeling left in my toes, no matter how much I move them around inside my boots. But I can't. Going inside feels a little bit like giving up. On helping Caroline. On finding Tom. And unraveling this whole awful night.

"Not yet," I say.

"But you're freezing."

"What do you think happened to Tom?" I ask, ignoring his statement.

"I think he ran away," Aiden says. "He knows that he fucked up big time, and he's doing his best to cover his tracks."

I shake my head.

"What's wrong?"

"I don't know, Aiden. I'm just so overwhelmed by everything. I mean, if I hadn't walked in on them...I don't think I could've ever believed that Tom, my friend Tom, was capable of doing anything like that. I mean, why would he? He's with Carrie. He loves her. At least, I think he does. And even if he doesn't, why would he do that to Caroline?"

"I don't know."

"He has always been too gentle and kind. I've never seen him hurt a fly. He has always been so sensitive. If anything, I thought he let girls walk all over him a little too much."

"The thing is that everyone has secrets. I mean, not everyone has secrets like Tom, but there are always things that we don't know about our friends and loved ones."

"I knew that he had some anger issues. He was really mad at me for rejecting him. And he said some awful things to me about my writing. But to do what he did to Caroline? I just never knew he was capable of that kind of evil."

Aiden shrugs. "Maybe he didn't know either. Maybe that was the first time he ever did anything like that."

"That's no excuse!"

"Yes, I know that. Of course not. But I'm just saying that maybe this was something new that he did. Maybe he didn't know he was capable of any of that either."

I stare at him, trying to figure out what he's saying.

"I'm not taking his side. Not at all, Ellie. I'm just trying to show you that maybe he hasn't been duplicitous the whole time you knew him. Maybe he just snapped."

I take in a deep breath and wait a few moments before letting it out. I don't know what to think. Maybe Aiden is right. Or maybe Tom has been this asshole the whole time I've known him and I was just completely blind to it. Who the hell knows? In either case, I want the police to find him and I want him to pay for what he did. He really hurt me. And not just me. He really hurt Caroline. He's a predator. A real predator. And I've been friends with him for years. I feel like such a fool.

"C'mon, let's take a walk." Aiden tugs on my shirt.

"No."

"C'mon, please?"

I sigh. I don't know what it is about being cold, but sometimes staying put and not actually moving a muscle feels warmer than standing up and letting the cold air engulf you completely. Aiden holds out his hand to me with a hopeful look on his face. I can't say no. Besides, a walk would be good for me. If

I can't bear to go back inside, I can at least stretch my legs out a little bit and get the blood moving through my body.

"Okay, fine." I finally cave and let him pull me up to my feet. I follow Aiden down the path between the cottages and back up around the other side of the house. At first, I think we're going to go down to the water, but instead we weave around the whole property going the long way around.

"Where are we going?" I ask.

"I don't know. We're just walking."

Holding on to his elbow, I put all of my weight on him. But he doesn't seem to mind. He's basically propping me up. I even close my eyes and let him lead me wherever he wants to. I'm utterly exhausted. I'm so tired that I don't want to be here anymore. I can't bear to. Instead, I just want to be as far away from here as possible - somewhere where people are kind, there is no pain, and the sun is shining and warm.

When we come around the bend toward the front of the Warrenhouse mansion, Aiden stops. Since he's leading me, I practically run into him. The jolt forces me to open my eyes. At the top of the stairs, I see the police officer who interviewed me, talking to Tom and Carrie and her parents.

All four of them are dressed in their pajamas and wearing thick robes on top of them. Tom, Carrie, and her mom are all wearing long coats and hats. Wait a second. What is going on here? I peer up the steps to make sure that I'm seeing everything right. I don't know about Mr. and Mrs. Warrenhouse or Carrie, but Tom should definitely not be wearing his pajamas. Or a hat. It's a small ski cap, but the way it's tugged so low around his head, it's covering up practically any sign of where I had hit him with that rock.

Tom sees me from the top of the stairs, but doesn't acknowledge me at all.

I'm about to go up the steps when Aiden pulls me back. There's another police officer standing in front and slightly to the side of us and his job seems to be to prevent anyone from going up the stairs.

"What's going on?" I ask Aiden. He shrugs.

Everyone on the porch is talking in such hushed tones that I can't hear a thing. So, we stand here watching and waiting. Why aren't they arresting him? Why are Carrie and her parents talking so much? The police officer is carefully taking notes just like he did with me, without making a move to put his handcuffs on Tom.

And then it hits me.

"Oh my God," I whisper to Aiden.

"What?"

"He's telling them that he was asleep the whole time," I say. "That's why he's dressed like that."

"He wasn't wearing pajamas before?"

"No, not at all. I mean, he was naked. But the clothes that I saw on the floor were what he wore to the party."

Aiden shrugs and shakes his head.

"I guess we'll just have to wait and see what happens," he says after a moment.

How can he remain so calm and patient? No, I need to stop this. I need to tell them that he's lying. And if Carrie is saying that he was with her, she's lying, too. I need to put a stop to this.

I make a move to go up the stairs, but the police officer at the bottom blocks me.

"May I help you, ma'am?"

"He's lying," I say loudly. "They're all lying."

"Lying about what?"

"I mean, I don't know exactly what they're saying but he was not wearing those clothes when I saw him. And if he's saying that he was asleep the whole time, that's a lie."

"Okay, ma'am," the cop says, continuing to prevent me from going up. "But we cannot allow you to interrupt the interview."

"What? I'm not going to interrupt anything."

"You have already given us your statement. Now, we're trying to get another statement."

"Even if it's a lie!" I say. Aiden puts his hand on my arm but I shrug him off. Why is no one believing me? What is going on?

"This is how we do things," the cop says after a while.

"They're going to figure it out," Aiden whispers in my ear, trying to push me away from the porch without much success. But I can't contain my anger and disbelief anymore.

"You have to ask him to take off his hat!" I scream loud enough for everyone on the porch to hear me. "I hit him with a rock in the temple. I'm sure it left a mark."

Tom shakes his head and says something to the police officer.

"Please, you have to believe me!" I scream louder.

"Ma'am, if you can't contain yourself, I'm going to have to put you in the back of the cruiser."

Aiden grabs me by the arm and pulls me away. "No, that won't be necessary. C'mon, Ellie. Let's let them do their job."

"But they're not doing their job," I say as he pulls me away. He's squeezing the top of my arm so hard that it's throbbing in pain. No matter what I do, I can't force him off me.

"Let me go!"

"Not until you calm down."

"I don't have to calm down."

"Yes, you do. Let them do their jobs. They're going to figure it out."

"No, they're going to believe him."

"Ellie, please. I don't want you to get arrested."

"I don't want to get arrested either."

"What do you think being put in the back of the cruiser means? Those doors don't open from the inside, you know," Aiden says, shaking me. He's holding me by my shoulders, trying to make me focus on him. But all I can see and hear is what's happening on that porch. I can't look away.

"I need them to know the truth," I say, burying my hands in my pockets and sulking. And then, it hits me. Yes, of course!

I run my fingers over Aiden's cell phone and everything becomes crystal clear. Suddenly, I remember that Tom still has my phone. He took it away from me. So, he must still have it. Of course, he may have left it in Caroline's cottage, but he may have taken it with him.

But wait, he's wearing different clothes. I doubt that he still has it on him. I look up at him and watch how expertly he is playing the part of the innocent man. The police officer is asking him questions, and he is shrugging and volunteering a lot of information. His shoulders are relaxed. His face doesn't have a single ounce of tension. Has he always been this good of an actor? Or did he just recently develop this skill?

I always thought that Tom was a good guy. I always thought that he was honest and hardworking. Maybe he was a little put upon, you know he worried a little too much about things that don't really matter. It's like he always carried the world on his shoulders. He wanted to be this perfect idea of a journalist that he imagined Ernest Hemingway was and he wanted to live up to someone else's fiction. He didn't see people as people, but as stories and illusions of who they were. He believed the myths and he always hated himself for being unable to live up to those myths.

But now, looking up at him standing on that porch, pretending that he did nothing wrong, that he was a complete innocent, I see a completely different man. He's no longer kind or sweet. He is just as self-absorbed, but not in the romantic way that I was once attracted to. He's not just cocky and confident. No, he's more of a psychopath. He is wearing a mask for the world and only I can see the truth. And Aiden, but that's only because he believes me. No, I have to do something to show his true self to everyone. Without that, the Warrenhouses will never believe me. And neither will Carrie. And despite my feelings about Carrie, she deserves to know the truth about the man she's about to marry.

"Excuse me!" I yell, running past Aiden and the cop positioned at the bottom of the porch. The only reason I'm able to sneak by is because both of them have let their guard down. And, by the time they realize what I'm doing, it's too late.

"Ma'am, you can't be here," the cop on the porch says to me. His voice is flat and calm. He's unnerved by my outburst. Carrie, Tom, and the Warrenhouses, on the other hand, all take a few steps away from me. As if they are afraid to catch my crazy.

"Ellie," Carrie says softly. "Can you please excuse us?"

This isn't the Carrie I know. She's quiet and reserved. This is the Carrie that she pretends to be around her parents.

I shake my head.

"No, I'm sorry."

"How can we help you, miss?" Mr. Warrenhouse asks. Out of the corner of my eye, I see Aiden's bewildered expression. Suddenly, I remember that his livelihood and the survival of Owl hangs in the balance. It's all up to Mr. Warrenhouse, or rather Robert. I don't want to screw that up. Of course not. But they deserve to know the truth.

"I don't know what Tom told you." I turn partly to the police officer and partly toward the Warrenhouses. Tom is standing a bit further apart, on the periphery, but still close enough to intimidate me.

I take a deep breath. "I don't know what Tom told you," I repeat myself. "Or why he's dressed in his pajamas and a robe, but I suspect that he is not telling you the truth."

"How so?" Mrs. Warrenhouse asks.

"I caught him...having sex with Caroline. She was unconscious. Passed out. And when I tried to call the police and report him, he took my phone away and attacked me."

"I did no such thing!" Tom says. "I was in bed with Carrie the whole time. Tell her!"

"Yes...he...was," Carries says tentatively. Her

statement isn't as confident or sure as it seemed before. I don't know if she's lying or just covering for him, but at this point I don't really care.

"Yes, you did," I say. "He wouldn't let me leave. When I finally got out of that cottage, he attacked me. I had to hit him with a rock just to break free."

"I have no idea what you're talking about." Tom laughs at me, shaking his head. I look at him and everyone else staring back at me. I have to make them believe me somehow.

"He probably has a mark someplace. I hit him pretty hard around the temple."

The police officer narrows his eyes. I see him scrutinizing Tom's appearance. "That's not true," Tom says.

"Well, in that case, you wouldn't mind taking off your hat, would you?" the cop asks. Tom's face loses all color. It's as if all the blood drains away from his face.

"Listen, I didn't tell you earlier because I had no idea she was going to make this kind of accusation. But I fell earlier."

The rhythm of his speech speeds up. He's looking for a way out. For a possible explanation for the mark that we both know is there.

"Please remove your hat," the cop says. We all wait. After a few moments of hesitation, he finally pulls it off. He runs his fingers through his limp messy hair, turning his right temple away from us. But no matter how much he tries to cover it up, it's there. As clear as daylight. There's a small cut and bruise, right next to his hairline.

Mrs. Warrenhouse gives out a little gasp.

"I slipped and fell last night. In the bathroom," Tom rattles off. "I had a little bit too much to drink. But then I was in bed with Carrie the whole night."

"Is that true, Carrie?" Mrs. Warrenhouse asks.

Carrie nods, looking down at the ground. She's avoiding eye contact with her mom and all of us. I can see that she's having doubts and isn't entirely sure at all. I glance over at the police officer. If he wasn't having doubts about Tom's story before, he is now.

"Did you say that he took your phone?" he asks after a moment.

"Yes, he did!" I say. Finally, I feel like I'm making some progress. All the doubts that he probably accumulated in his head are finally starting to add up to something bigger.

I take out Aiden's phone from my pocket.

"What are you doing?" Carrie asks.

"I'm going to call my phone."

"I don't have your phone, Ellie," Tom says. "I have no idea why you're doing this. I thought you were my friend."

This makes me mad. He's using our friendship to appeal to my sense of empathy. He's trying to manipulate me. I read that in an article about psychopaths before. That's their go-to strategy. Normal people have friendships and relationships, and if they are involved with a psychopath in their life, then they are easily manipulated because the psychopath sees nothing wrong with pulling at their heart strings to get what they want.

"I thought you were my friend, Tom. I thought you

were Caroline's. I never expected you to do that to her."

"I didn't do anything to her, Ellie. You're—"

"I'm not wrong," I interrupt him.

"No, you're just...mistaken."

I stare at him. Is he really saying this? The confidence in his voice is unnerving. If I didn't know the truth, I would be tempted to believe him. Wow. Shivers run down my spine. He's actually giving me chills.

"No, I'm not." I dial my number on Aiden's phone. Please be somewhere around here, I say to myself. It has to be around here.

Of course, I wouldn't put it past Tom to hide the phone somewhere where no one would find it. Maybe even toss it into the ocean. But I pray that he didn't think it through that much.

We all wait for a few moments, but we don't hear anything. After a few minutes, it goes to voice mail. Shit.

"No, no, no. He took my phone," I insist. "Please, you

have to believe me."

The police officer shakes his head. "It's fine. I do," he says unconvincingly.

But that's not good enough. I dial the number again. Again, we all wait to hear something. Anything.

"Okay, miss, let me finish talking to these people here, okay?" the police officer says to me. "I already have your statement."

He is escorting me away from them. "If we need anything else from you, I will be in touch."

He walks me all the way down the stairs and hands me over to Aiden. Aiden puts his arm around my shoulders and gives me a reassuring hug.

"It's going to be okay. They'll figure it out," he whispers in my ear. But somehow, that doesn't make me feel any better. They don't believe me now and there's nothing I can do about it. I feel tears welling up in my eyes. My throat closes up as I gasp for breath. I've become overcome with emotion and regret and there's nothing I can do to stop any of it. No one believes me. At least no one who really should. Aiden wraps his arms around me and wipes the tears that stream out of my eyes.

"You're okay. You're okay," he whispers over and over.

My nose starts to run and no matter how much I inhale and try to keep it all inside my throat and mouth, all the goop starts to come out. Gross. I turn my face away from Aiden and everyone else as I continue to ugly cry.

Somewhere, in between my gasps for air, I hear the front door to the house open. Through the tears, I can't quite make out what's going on. But as I wipe them away and slow down my breathing somewhat, I realize that there's another police officer up on the porch with them. He's not the one who I spoke to and he isn't the one who blocked my entrance to the porch. No, this is someone entirely new. I've never seen him before.

"What's going on?" I ask Aiden. He shrugs.

We watch as the police officer, the new one who is wearing blue latex gloves, shows the other one something. They both turn to face me.

"Is this your phone, miss?" he asks, holding up my phone with a light pink glittery cover.

"Yes! It is. Where did you find it?" I exclaim.

"In Ms. Warrenhouse's room," he says. Carrie shakes her head, stepping away from Tom.

"Carrie, no, this is some sort of misunderstanding," he says, grabbing her hand. But she shakes it off and walks away from him.

"Please, you have to believe me."

Tom continues to beg and plead, but it's all to no avail. Carrie and her parents extricate themselves from him and go inside. Tom tries to follow them inside, but the police officer who took my statement takes him by the arm and escorts him down the stairs toward his cruiser.

"What's going on? Am I under arrest?"

"We need to ask you more questions at the station, Tom," the cop says, holding his head down as he puts him in the back of his cruiser.

"You bitch!" Tom yells at me as he slams the door shut.

I inhale and exhale deeply as I feel the weight of the world lift off my shoulders. Aiden turns me around to face him. He buries his hands in my hair and tugs slightly, relieving all the pressure that has built up.

"Mmm-mmm," I moan.

"You're amazing," he says, pressing his lips onto mine. Slowly, he parts my lips and runs his tongue over mine. Whatever tension remains in my body, all but dissipates.

"I love you," I whisper.

"I love you, too."

CHAPTER 13 - ELLIE

*I*nstead of returning to the cottage and getting some sleep, Aiden and I decide to go straight to the hospital to see about Caroline. Despite the fact that I didn't get a minute of shut-eye last night, I know that there's no way that I could get any rest without seeing her first. I have to know if she's alright.

Instead of calling another driver to take us there, Aiden made a few calls and a sleek, brand new silver BMW arrived for him to use direct from the local rental place. I had no idea that you could even rent a car without going to the lot, but I guess anything is possible for the right price.

On the way over, Aiden and I don't really talk. I find

a pop station on the radio and turn it up. Out of the corner of my eye, I see the sour expression on his face. It feels like it's about something more than what just happened with Tom and the police. Something more visceral. Primal even.

"What's wrong?" I ask.

"No, nothing." He shrugs it off.

"Tell me," I insist. "Are you worried about Caroline?"

"Well, yes, of course I am."

"But your facial expression, just now, it's not about that is it?"

He flashes a coy smile at me.

"Are you hungry? Do you want to drive through Starbucks on the way?"

"Yes, definitely. But don't change the subject."

"Okay, fine. I'm not a huge fan of pop music."

Hmm. I'm actually taken aback by this.

"And by not being a huge fan, I mean, I hate it."

I look over at him. He actually looks a little proud in announcing this.

"What are you talking about?" I ask, shaking my head. "You mean, you don't like...who? Beyonce? Taylor Swift? Bruno Mars?"

Aiden shakes his head definitively. "No, I don't."

"None of them? Or just one or two?" I ask. I still can't believe what I'm hearing. Are these words actually coming out of his mouth?

"Let's just say that I'm more of a rock 'n roll kind of guy," he says, shrugging.

I stare at him. Dumbfounded.

"Close your mouth, dear," Aiden says, joking. He reaches out and physically lifts my chin up to the rest of the mouth.

"I'm just shocked. I mean...I don't even understand the words that you are saying."

"Well, what can I say?"

"So, what kind of music do you like then?"

"Um, let's see. The classics mainly. Old bands. You

know, Led Zeppelin, Yard Birds, the Rolling Stones. I have a bunch of their records at home."

"Records?"

"Yep, I'm pretty old school."

"Don't you need a turn table, too?" I ask. "Or whatever that's called."

"Yep, and I've got that, too."

I shake my head and laugh as we pull into the Starbucks drive-through. Luckily, pumpkin spice lattes are still in season because I don't think I can handle any more surprises today. I also order a breakfast wrap.

"Do you want me to put something else on?" I ask as we pull away with our hot drinks and breakfasts in hand.

"No, it's fine. I'm just warning you...for the future."

I laugh. "Well, speaking of the future, I'm not sure how I feel about being involved with someone who doesn't like Beyonce."

"Oh, really?" Aiden raises his eyebrows. "Well, we're

in agreement then. I'm not sure how I feel about being involved with someone who does."

We take a sip of our drinks and break out laughing. As we pull into the hospital parking lot, I suddenly realize that I really needed this. A break from all the doom and gloom.

"This is nice," I say. "It's a nice break from everything else that happened today. Oh my God, I can't believe how long this day has been already."

"I can't even imagine," Aiden says. "I mean, at least I got some sleep. But you...you must be exhausted."

Yep, bing, bing, bing. In fact, I'm more than exhausted. I'm actually shocked that I"m still standing up straight. I've been up for more hours than I can count and haven't laid down once since the party. And given everything that happened, and how much sleep I require just to function like a normal person, I'm pretty sure that once I do go to sleep, I will be asleep for a very, very long time.

Once we pull into the hospital parking lot, the mood in the car grows more serious. Neither of us know what to say or what to expect. I'm just glad that

Aiden is here for me. I don't think I could go in there all by myself.

"I hate hospitals," I say on our walk over. "Actually, I'm sort of terrified of them."

"You are?"

"Well, I've never even been in one. I mean, not overnight or for any other reason. So I just sort of associate them...with bad things."

"Yes, bad things happen in hospitals. But good things happen, too. People get better."

I think about that for a moment. "Do you think Caroline will?"

"Yes, I do," he says quickly. I don't know if he said it that way as a show of confidence or if he actually believes it. But I hope to God that he's right.

When we get inside, Aiden takes charge and asks the nurses about Caroline. He gives them all of Caroline's info. Even though we are not technically family, he sweet talks them into letting us through. Besides, Caroline's family isn't anywhere near Maine and I'm the closest thing to family that they have.

The younger, doe-eyed nurse who looks like she has been working for a full twelve-hour shift already shows us to her room. I follow behind Aiden all up to the point where we reach her room, and then he turns around and pushes me forward.

"She'll want to see you first," he whispers in my ear. Before I know what's going on, I find myself inside. The lighting is harsh and unpleasant, but the smile that pops up on Caroline's face when she sees me is genuine and bright.

"Oh my God." I run over to her and grab her hand. I try not to squeeze too hard, but I can't help myself. I can't even believe that she's awake. And alive.

"How are you? Are you okay?"

Caroline shakes her head with great difficulty. "I'm good," she whispers. Her voice is raspy and forced. She's clearly not good, but even in this state she's in much better shape than I ever imagined she would be. I mean, yes, of course, I was remaining positive and optimistic. But it wasn't until I actually saw her alive and smiling that I realized just how lost I thought she was.

I hug her and squeeze her hand and she continues to

smile at me. When I finally pull away, my eyes are brimming in tears and I turn away to wipe them.

"You're such a crybaby," she says, smiling.

"I know," Aiden says. "Has she always been this way?"

"Pretty much."

"I was just so worried about you," I say quickly. "I just saw you lying there..."

I can't bear to finish the statement. It's all too much and tears well up in my eyes again. I turn away from her and bury my head in Aiden's shoulder. I feel like such an idiot. And a child. Here I am bawling my eyes out in front of someone who actually suffered. She was the one who went through all that and I'm the one who is begging for attention. But of course, that's not true. Attention is the last thing I want. My heart is just aching for my friend and I want to take all her pain away, but unfortunately, I can't. When I finally compose myself enough to turn around, Caroline clears her throat and points to something on the nearby table. I don't know what she means, but Aiden does. He walks over immediately and hands her the large jug with a straw. Caroline takes a few sips of water and wets her lips. I notice how cracked and brittle they are. Almost bleeding from being so dry.

"Do you want some Chapstick? Or gloss?" I ask.

"No, not right now. Thanks. They have just been pumping me with so many drugs that it really dried everything out."

Caroline takes another few sips and licks her lips for good measure.

"The cops were here earlier," she says after a moment.

"They were?" I ask.

"Two of them. One was a detective. He wanted to talk to me right after I woke up."

"How did it go?" Aiden asks.

"Well, I was still pretty groggy. Not entirely sure what I said to him."

"What do you mean?" I ask.

She shrugs. "I'm just kidding. Of course."

I smile.

"They did a rape kit," she adds.

I nod. I want to know more about it, like what exactly did that entail. But I don't know if she's in the mood to talk about it. And I don't want to do anything to make this process worse. I try to think of some polite way to go about talking to her about all of this.

"So...what do you remember about last night?" I ask. "That is, if you want to talk about it at all. Because you totally don't have to."

Caroline cracks a smile.

"Your girlfriend is pretty neurotic, you know that?" she asks Aiden. He smiles at her.

"Yes, I'm getting that sense."

None of us say anything for a few moments. I think that Aiden and I just wait for her to continue, in any way that she sees fit.

"The thing is that I don't remember much," she says after a minute. "Taylor and I got into a fight."

"Taylor?" Aiden asks. "The guy you met on my yacht?"

"Yes. The guy who I thought was a nice guy, but then I caught him flirting with another girl. When I made a scene, another girl came up to me and said that he gave her his number earlier in the night."

"Oh my God, that's awful," I say.

"Well, you know, that's what you get for trying to date a rich asshole who would buy a woman at an auction, right?" Caroline says, rolling her eyes. It takes her a moment to remember herself.

"Oh, I'm sorry. I didn't mean that. Present company excluded, of course," she says to Aiden.

"None taken." He shrugs and flashes a wide smile. "I get it. Totally."

"So what happened then?" I ask.

"Well, I was drowning my sorrows at the bar. Tom came over. We started talking about this and that. His issues with Carrie and her parents. Then we decided to go somewhere more private, to one of the rooms at the other end of the house. When I finished my drink, he offered to bring me another."

Okay, so far, nothing bad happened, I say to myself. So, how the hell did it all go so wrong?

"Well, that's when things get a little blurry," Caroline says. "After I had that other drink, I didn't feel very good. And Tom helped me back to my room. And I don't remember anything after that."

"Nothing?" I ask.

"No."

I feel all color drain from my face.

"What happened?" Caroline asks.

I don't want to tell her, but she deserves to know the truth. Aiden nudges me a little.

I take a deep breath and tell her what I saw. Every detail. I want to gloss over some, but I don't dare. She needs to know everything. At least, everything that I saw.

Caroline listens carefully. By the look on her face I can tell that she doesn't quite yet fully grasp what I'm saying.

"So, you saw him on top of me?" she asks after a while. I nod.

"And I was passed out?"

"Yes." I nod again. I don't know how to make this better, but she has to know the truth.

"I guess that's why the cops were here. And why they wanted to do the rape kit," she says absentmindedly. I nod again. She turns away from me. I pick up her hand. A single tear runs down her cheek.

CHAPTER 14 - ELLIE

THE NUMBNESS AFTER THE FACT...

*D*riving back from the hospital, Aiden and I aren't sure what we should do. He wants to go back to New York as soon as possible. He says that he has a lot of work to get back to. But I know that he also wants to get back home because things have become rather complicated here. I mean, we are staying at the home of the people whose future son-in-law I just accused of rape. Don't get me wrong. I want to go back home, too. Nothing would make me happier. But then there's Caroline. She's going to be in the hospital until at least tomorrow and I just don't feel right leaving her. She is far from home, in a state she has never been to. I called her parents while I was at the hospital, but they won't be able to come up until tomorrow.

"I just don't feel right leaving her," I say to Aiden. "I guess you can go back to New York."

"No, I'm not letting you stay at that house all alone."

"Tom's not there," I say. The thought of staying at the house sends shivers through me. I don't want to stay there myself. Too many bad memories. Besides, I'm not the biggest fan of Carrie Warrenhouse on a good day.

"But, no, I don't really want to stay there," I say after a moment.

"Let's get a hotel," Aiden says.

"What?"

"If you want to stay here to see Caroline more, that's fine. I can do some work here. I just don't want to stay at their house."

I smile at him. That's perfect. The last thing I want to do is go back to that cottage ever again, let alone stay there. But we do have to get our things, at the very least.

We arrive back the Warrenhouses' estate half an hour later and head straight into our cottage. I pack up my bag, secretly thankful that I didn't bring that much stuff. It takes Aiden less than a minute to get all of his. I do one last sweep of the place, including checking the bathroom and all the counters in case I forgot something. I already did a routine check of the outlets because I'm one to always forget a charger.

"So, what should we do now?" I ask after I put my bag next to Aiden's near the front door. I know that we need to tell the Warrenhouses that we're leaving, but I really don't want to. I barely know them as it is and things are quite awkward with Carrie already. She was my boss not too long ago and I did quit without much of a warning. I know that I had good reasons. I suddenly had money and she had been annoying me for way too long. But still, what happened last night is the last thing in the world that I expected.

"We could leave and just call from the road or the hotel," Aiden says. "But I think that would be a little rude."

I nod. He's right, of course.

"They did invite us to their party and they didn't

have anything to do with what happened to Caroline."

I nod again. I know all of this. Still, it doesn't make any of it any easier. A feeling of utter dread descends upon me as I come closer and closer to the eventuality of talking to them again.

"And Robert is very interested in investing in Owl," Aiden adds. By the tone of his voice, I can tell that he's doing his best in trying to convince himself to go talk to them as much as he's trying to convince me.

"Yes, you can't jeopardize that," I say decidedly. As far as I can tell, Robert Warrenhouse is Aiden's Hail Mary. He's the only thing that can save Owl from falling apart. He's also the only thing that can probably save Aiden from losing his job.

"C'mon, let's just say good-bye and then we can get some rest," I say as Aiden looks down at his feet to avoid eye contact with me.

He sighs deeply as we walk out to our car with our bags.

"You really don't want to see them?" I ask, handing him my suitcase.

"No, it's not that," he says with a shrug. "I just hate feeling like this. So, useless. Impotent even."

I nod.

"The thing is I've run this company since I started it. All of the decisions have always been mine. Everything we did was up to me. I didn't really need anyone before. At least, I thought I didn't. And then, Blake did that. Basically ruined my whole business. And now, I find myself in this completely weak and insecure position. I need to go around begging people for money just so I can go back to doing my job."

"I'm so sorry."

"It's just total shit, Ellie. I didn't do anything wrong. I mean, maybe I trusted him too much. But I didn't actually screw anyone over. And if the investors had just stayed put, they would have a lot more money in another year. We were on a trajectory to really blow away the competition. Like Facebook when they went public."

I nod and put my arm around him. I wish there were something I could do. But just like him, I feel completely helpless. In addition to feeling helpless, I also feel like it's all my fault.

"I'm just so sorry about everything that happened," I say after a moment of silence. "I can't help but feel like it's all my fault."

"Your fault?" Aiden looks up at me. "What are you talking about?"

"I don't know. I shouldn't have participated in that auction. I had a feeling that something was wrong."

"No, I was the one who was wrong. I thought it would be fun. Sexy. And now, I just feel like such a fool. I had no idea he would do any of that. I had no idea what an asshole Blake really is. Agh, it makes me so angry," Aiden says, clenching his fists. "I feel like I could just punch something."

I put my hand on the small of his back and rub him a little.

"C'mon, let's just be nice and say good-bye. Get this over with," I say.

CHAPTER 15 - ELLIE

QUESTIONS LEFT UNASWERED...

*T*knock on the front door, but no one answers. I knock again and wait. Only after I ring the doorbell, do I hear footsteps on the other side. Carrie answers the door.

"Hey, how are you?" I ask. My voice is flat and mechanical. I just want to get through this and go to the hotel and get some rest.

"We just wanted to thank you and your parents for having us and let you know that we're going to go to a hotel," I say without waiting for an answer.

"Oh, okay," Carrie says quietly. She is dressed in a large puffy sweater and sweatpants. Her eyes are bloodshot and her skin is so pale, I can see the blue veins underneath.

"I'm really sorry about everything, Carrie," I add. She nods and looks away, wrapping her arms around her shoulders.

"Yeah, me, too," she says after a moment.

I feel like I need to say something else. But another part of me is urging me to leave. We stopped by. We said our good-byes. Why stick around? Lingering can only make things worse.

"Is Tom still with the police?" I ask before I can stop myself.

Carrie nods and shrugs. Aiden tugs on my shirt slightly. "We should go," he whispers.

I turn around to leave, but then Carrie says, "The thing is that I still don't really understand what happened."

Shit, I say to myself.

"What do you mean?" I ask.

"I'm just confused about the whole thing. I mean,

are you sure that you saw him doing that? Tom isn't...like that you know?"

"Yes, I know. I was surprised, too."

"I mean, you know him. He's a really sweet person."

I stare at her. I don't really know how to respond to this. A part of me understands where she's coming from. But I also know what I saw. And it was Tom. And he was doing horrible things to Caroline.

"Listen, thank you for having us," Aiden says. "Please tell your parents thank you as well."

I can tell that Aiden is anxious to get out of here. But before we can make our escape, Mr. and Mrs. Warrenhouse show up at the door.

"We just wanted to stop by and say good-bye," I say to them. "We're going to stay at a hotel in town. But thank you so much for having us. You have a beautiful home."

"Thank you for coming," Mrs. Warrenhouse says absentmindedly. It's the morning after and all traces of the perfectly put-together chic woman in impossible high heels with the gorgeous waist and hair are gone. Instead, she is dressed in a comfortable pair of leggings, a large oversized sweater, and slippers. She looks tired and worn out. And not just from the party.

"Tom is doing well," Mr. Warrenhouse says to Carrie. "I just got off the phone with his lawyer."

I stare at him. Did he really just say that? Did those words really just come out of his mouth? I don't know if he had forgotten about us or doesn't really care that we hear.

"Are you sure?" Carrie asks hopefully. "Do you think it's going to be okay?"

"Well, no guarantees, of course," Mr. Warrenhouse says. "But I got him set up with one of my most experienced lawyers. Plus, Tom's not an idiot. His father's an attorney."

I glance over at Aiden. He looks just as shocked as I do.

"Wait a second, I don't understand," I say. "Why are you taking Tom's side? I mean, I know he's your fiancé, but what about what he did to Caroline?"

"Honey, we know that you strongly believe in what you saw. But you weren't there the whole time," Mrs. Warrenhouse says to me. "You don't know how it all happened."

I take a step back. Suddenly, she doesn't look so helpless and broken anymore. She's embodying her position as a matriarch and taking care of her family. I hate the fact that I ever felt bad for her.

"With all due respect, Tom was the attacker. It doesn't matter what happened before. Caroline was passed out so she couldn't possibly give her consent."

"We know that's what you believe, honey," she says in her most disgustingly sweet voice. "But the thing is that life isn't black and white like that."

"I just don't understand why you're taking his side. I mean, do you want your daughter to marry someone like that? Someone who rapes women?"

"Tom did not rape that girl," Mr. Warrenhouse says definitively. I really thought that he would at least be on Caroline's side, but now it's clear to me that this whole family is fucked.

"Yes, he did, Robert," Aiden says, taking a step closer to me. My heart skips a beat. He's on my side. It feels so good to have someone on my side.

"I don't think it's a good time to discuss this. We have all had very little sleep and the night has been very stressful," Mrs. Warrenhouse says. "Thank you for coming."

"Okay," I mumble. Aiden takes me by the arm and we walk down the steps off their porch.

"Oh, and, Aiden," Mr. Warrenhouse yells after us. "I'm sorry, but given everything that's happened, I don't think it would be wise for me to invest in Owl at this time. I wish you all the best with your future ventures."

I can't help but drop Aiden's hand. When I reach for it again, Aiden pushes my hand away. I can see the disappointment and sadness on his face, but he quickly composes himself.

"Thank you for your time and consideration," he says slowly. Wow, what a class act. I want him to run up there and yell at the Warrenhouses and maybe even punch them. But what would that accomplish?

Nothing. He doesn't want to invest in Owl and there's not much we can do about it.

Aiden unlocks the car and holds the door open for me. A few minutes later, we speed away from this place as quickly as we can.

CHAPTER 16 - AIDEN

WHEN DISAPPOINTMENTS PILE UP...

 don't want Ellie to know just how pissed off I am.

I try to hold it back.

I try to push it somewhere dark within me - to that same deep place where I put all of my dark thoughts.

But I'm only partly successful. Robert Warrenhouse pulling out of Owl is one of the biggest blows I've ever suffered. It's nearly as horrible as Blake pulling out in the first place. But what makes this even more painful is that we finally had a chance. We had an opportunity to get back to where we were. My mind shifts to all of those employees who work for me.

What will they do if Owl goes under?

How will they find new jobs?

They'll have to move somewhere else. They'll have to take their kids out of school. Their whole lives will be destroyed.

And for what?

What exactly did I do wrong?

I stood up to Blake for what he did to Ellie; and I stood up for Ellie's account of what Tom did to Caroline.

Even though all of this happened because Ellie is in my life, I don't blame her.

Not one bit.

If it weren't for her my life wouldn't be nearly as great now, despite all this shit that I'm dealing with. No. She put my life in perspective.

Suddenly, I know what's important. I know what's valuable.

Before, I was this successful playboy without much to show for anything. I knew how to have a good time, but that was pretty much it. Now, it feels like I have a family again.

I glance over at Ellie out of the corner of my eye as I drive to the hotel. I want to go back to New York, back to work.

But, for what?

What do I even have to go back to?

Robert Warrenhouse was my last shot. My last opportunity. No other single investor has that much money to play around with and institutional investors aren't going to touch Owl with a hundred-mile pole, if there were such a thing. No, without a huge infusion of cash, Owl is pretty much over. The Board of Directors will want my head on a spike to save face in front of the shareholders and they're entitled to it.

They'll give me a generous severance package, of course, and appoint someone else as CEO. That person will do his or her best to save Owl, but without going into advertising and trying to save the company by having it make money somehow, and not just be a free service, there won't be much anyone will be able to do.

The only thing I don't know is exactly how long we will hold on. Will it be a slow decline into obsolescence like what happened to America Online or will we fall straight down to the bottom in a fiery crash like MySpace?

"Are you okay?" Ellie asks, putting my hand over hers.

I shrug and force a smile. My thoughts are running a mile a minute, one over another.

One moment, I want to scream and punch someone for what Blake and Robert have done to me and the next, all I can think about is all the people who work for me and what they're going to do next. I will still have money.

Not as much as before, not a billionaire anymore.

But, who cares?

I don't live on a salary of eighty thousand dollars a year like many of my engineers. And then there are the secretaries and the lower-grade employees.

They are single mothers and fathers who support their kids on salaries as small as thirty or forty thousand a year.

What the hell are they going to do?

How much will all of this affect them?

When this thought pops into my head, that's when my disappointment and hopelessness really turns into anger and fury.

Who the hell does Blake think he is for doing what he's doing to Owl?

And it's all because he had his pride hurt a little bit. He did something wrong and a girl stood up to him.

All because of that, he's acting like the douche that I should've known him to be all along.

"Fuck him," I say, gritting through my teeth.

"What?"

I didn't realize that that came out aloud. But if I can't talk about this with Ellie, who can I talk about this with?

"I'm just so pissed at Blake. And Robert," I say. "I mean, less so Robert, I guess. Since he didn't really sign anything and his lawyers didn't go over any of Owl's internal documents yet. But, still. He's just pulling out because he's taking Tom's side. And for what? Why the hell is he taking Tom's side? What a dick."

"I know, right? I mean, I thought that they would be happy that they found out the truth about who Tom was before their daughter married him. But I guess not."

"The thing is that some people don't want to know the truth. They just want to live in their little bubble. They'd rather pretend that everything is okay than come face to face with facts."

Ellie nods and a tear rolls down her cheek.

"What's wrong?" I ask.

"I'm just sad. I mean, you didn't know Tom. But there was a lot of good about him. Of course, what he did is unforgivable. But I just don't even understand how the hell it happened. Or why. I mean, we were friends for a very long time. We were really close. And he never showed himself to be someone who is capable of anything like this."

"Some people just snap, I guess," I say. "I never thought Blake would do anything like what he did on the yacht either."

She nods. Little does she know, but I know exactly what she's feeling right now. I knew Blake was a bit of a chauvinist and an asshole, but I had no idea he was capable of anything that he did on the yacht with Ellie. He took it too far, and finding out something like that about your friend is devastating. To say the least.

"So, what are we going to do now?" she asks.

"I don't know," I say, pulling into the parking lot. "Get some sleep, I guess."

"Sleep sounds like heaven," Ellie says.

I thought this would be a hotel, but it's actually an inn. The Poplar Inn, to be exact. It has a white picket fence, a wraparound porch, and thick pine trees all around.

An older woman comes out to greet us as soon as we come up onto the porch. She welcomes us in and tells us what time we can expect breakfast the following morning.

CHAPTER 17 - ELLIE

*A*iden carries our bags into the room. It's not modern in the least, but it is incredibly charming. The walls are covered in flowery wallpaper and the dresser and the nightstands are covered with way too many knickknacks.

This room was definitely decorated by an older woman with a little too many doilies to find homes for, but there's something sweet about it as well.

Plus, the view.

Wow, the view is amazing.

I walk up to the large bay window and stare at the brooding ocean just outside. The clouds have swept in, as if to tell us that there's nothing good out in the world for today and we need to just stay put.

"Isn't the ocean beautiful?" I ask as Aiden walks up to me and puts his arms around me.

"Yes," he whispers. "But not as beautiful as you."

A big smile comes over my face. I try to push it aside, but my lips just part without my consent.

"I want you," he whispers in my ear, nibbling at the outer edge a bit. Shivers run down my spine. Suddenly, within a moment, all those thoughts I had on our way over here disappear. It's not that I'm not concerned about what's going to happen with everything in the future, it's that I just don't really care about it right now.

"I want you, too," I say. Without fully realizing what I'm doing, I just let my body do what it wants. I sink down to my knees on the carpeted floor. I pull down his pants. Not all the way down, but just enough to access the goods.

Aiden exhales deeply with his whole body.

"Ellie—" he starts to say, but I stop him.

"Shhh," I say.

I wrap my hands around his hard penis and lick the top. He reaches back and steadies himself a little with the chair behind him.

I close my eyes and hold him close. I put the head in my mouth and start to suck gently. The softness of his skin makes me moan. I lose myself in the intoxicating way that he smells.

I speed up a little, his whole body starting to shake. It starts like a ripple, but quickly becomes something more powerful like a vibration.

"Ellie, this is...amazing," he says slowly. The words barely come out as I continue to work on him.

"Does it feel good?" I whisper through the licks. I flutter my tongue across the underneath part and feel as my own body shivers from the arousal and delight.

I want this to last for a long time. I want to make him wait for it.

"God...Ellie. Your mouth. You're amazing. Keep doing that. Just like that," he moans, tossing his head back.

I get so turned on by his pleasure that I feel myself getting wet. His hands make their way down my throat and toward my breasts.

He rubs my nipples over and over in the same rhythm as I suck on him.

I love how slowly it started out and how aroused and hard he got in a matter of moments.

I feel in control, but I can't make it last. I want him to orgasm. I want to put him over the edge.

My head bobs up as I pleasure him, stroking him with one hand and tugging and pulling on him with my mouth. I lick the veins that pop out of his hard cock and I slide my tongue over them, outlining them.

Just when I think Aiden can't get any bigger, he continues to swell and grow even thicker and longer. I look up at him occasionally and watch how much pleasure I'm giving him. He thrusts his hips in and out and I wrap my hands around his perfect ass.

"I'm getting close," he moans without opening his eyes.

A part of me wants to make him wait. To tease him,

just like he teased me. But I can't wait myself. I'm completely stripped to my basic needs and the only thing I can think of is how I can make him orgasm and how good it's going to be.

No, I'm not as strong as him. I can't contain my excitement the same way. The thought of him reaching his climax in my mouth makes me crazed. I feel greedy and I don't care.

I grip his butt even more and move my head faster and faster. I'm becoming frantic. He moans louder and louder. My jaw starts to feel sore, but I work through the pain. I'm desperate for his climax. I need it like I have never needed anything before.

The first spurt comes so quickly that it catches me off guard. I struggle to swallow. Aiden continues to thrust against the back of my throat with his cock throbbing inside of my mouth with each pulsation. His body starts to shake as I take everything he has. His moans become louder and louder, but become muddled when he runs out of breath.

After the first few thrusts, Aiden collapses on the arm chair behind him, and I continue to lick him until he's clean. His large cock doesn't soften a bit and moves up and down a bit to meet my mouth. His cock is definitely ready to fuck me if I want it, but when I look up at his face, I can see that he is fully spent.

"Oh... my... God... Ellie," Aiden finally manages to utter.

"Was that good?" I ask coyly, wiping my mouth and getting up from my knees. He nods frantically and I smile.

"Good," I say and head to the bed. I don't want anything from him in return. I just wanted that. And now, I need to rest.

It takes Aiden a few moments to gather himself. But within a few minutes, he plops down on the bed next to me with a loud thump. He runs his fingers along my arm and gives me a little peck on the back of my hand.

CHAPTER 18 - ELLIE

AFTER SOME SLEEP…

I don't remember falling asleep, but it's pitch black when I finally wake up. I wake up late in the evening with Aiden asleep next to me.

My stomach is grumbling in pain. I haven't eaten anything since this morning's Starbucks.

As I try to run over everything that has happened, I get a headache and decide to give up instead. There's no point in thinking about all that right now.

I stretch my arms out and sit up. What I do actually need now is a glass of water. I walk over to the bathroom and cup some water into my mouth.

My lips are so dry they are practically bleeding and my throat is completely parched. I feel like I haven't drunk an ounce of water in weeks.

I continue to scoop water into my mouth until I'm completely full. When I'm finally done, I look up at myself in the mirror. Not a pretty sight. My eyes are barely open and somewhat swollen on top of that.

Whatever little makeup I was wearing is either gone or completely smeared in the most unattractive way. I splash water on my face and rub my eyes for good measure.

After wiping my face with the towel, I finally feel a little more awake. Still very tired, but at least somewhat like a human being.

When I walk back over to the bed, Aiden opens his eyes and smiles at me. I can still smell him on me and the aroma is intoxicating.

Without a word, he reaches out to me and pulls me back into bed. I try to resist, but it's to no avail. He kisses me slowly and deeply, savoring every moment.

My hands slide down his back. He isn't wearing a

shirt anymore and my hand makes its way down his muscular back. As he pushes himself closer to me, I realize that he's actually completely nude.

"Hi," Aiden whispers.

I smile at him.

"I want you to come for me now," he says.

His voice is deep and sexy, full of decadence. Every part of my body tingles.

He doesn't just want me to come; he wants me to come *for* him. As if on command. My heart flutters.

"Oh, is that so?" I ask.

He reaches down and wraps his powerful hand around my butt cheeks, squeezing them and lifting me on top of him.

"Yes." He nods.

I run my fingers over his hair. Each strand is smooth, soft, and thick. When I tug lightly, he gives off a moan.

He slides down my body and nuzzles his face between my breasts. He pulls off my top and pulls down the cup of my bra. I gasp as his mouth wraps around my nipple. He tugs and pulls and I can't help but toss my head back in pleasure.

"Do you trust me?" he asks. I open my eyes and look down at him.

"What do you mean?"

"I want to try something new. A bit different. But I think you're going to love it."

My heart skips a beat. What could he mean? But before I can make a decision one way or another, I nod.

Aiden gets off the bed and walks over to the table at the far end of the room. He comes back with scissors, which he fishes out of the top drawer.

"What are you doing?" I ask.

He smiles.

"You said you trust me."

"I do. But, with scissors?" I ask, skeptically.

He walks over to me and gets back into bed. Then he brings the scissors to my breasts.

My heart jumps into my throat, but I know that there's no way he would actually hurt me. So, I wait for him to do as he pleases.

"I will get you another bra," he says and lifts up the lacy portion and starts to cut.

I watch carefully as he carefully cuts out the cup, leaving the straps and everything else in place. Once he's done with one side, he takes that breast into his mouth and sucks gently, sending me into a throw of ecstasy.

But he does not stay here for long. Instead, he turns his attention to my other breast. After a few moments, the cups of my bra are gone and my breasts stand erect and exposed before him. I'm still wearing the bra but it's not doing much besides outlining my breasts.

"Now, that's better," Aiden says, putting the scissors on the nightstand and taking my breasts into his hands.

He nuzzles in between them and licks and tugs until I'm ready to scream out. I arch my back into him with pleasure and he pins my hands to the bed.

Slowly, one of his hands makes its way down my body toward my core.

"You're all wet and swollen for me," he whispers, pulling my panties to one side.

I nod and open my legs.

He pulls me closer, over his shoulders, and licks me between my folds. His mouth is soft and provocative on my sensitive flesh.

I grab a hold of the sheets and squeeze them in between my fingers.

My jaw tenses up.

My breathing gets faster and faster. His tongue circles my clit at the top and nudges me just right. My hips start to move as if on their own.

"Oh, Aiden," I moan. But then he pulls away.

"Not yet," he says firmly.

He is torturing me and he knows it. I both love and hate him for it. He is taking me to the brink of orgasm and not letting me go completely.

A thin layer of sweat forms all over my body. It feels

like the next stroke of his hand or tongue will set me off, but I try to hold on.

Right before I let go completely, he pulls away.

Again.

I gasp and moan in disappointment.

But instead of just coming right back, he gets up.

"Where are you going?" I ask, shaking my head.

No, this can't be over.

Not yet.

I need to come.

He can't just leave me hanging.

"You said you would trust me," Aiden says, taking my hands and pulling me off the bed.

He leads me over to the large chair with rounded arm rests. I think he's going to sit me down in it, but instead he spins me around and bends me over it.

He leaves for a moment and then comes back with a scarf, which he ties around my hands and the back of the chair.

It's not particularly tight, but the experience sends shivers through my body. I'm still wearing my bra, but my naked nipples are pressed tightly around the leather. When he has me in place, he gives me a little slap on my butt.

"Oh, wow, you're so hot, Ellie," Aiden whispers.

Except for my lacy panties, my ass is completely exposed to him. That's all I am at this moment and it never felt so arousing.

Slowly, Aiden pulls down my panties. When he reaches the bottom of my legs, I step out of them.

"That's a good girl," he says, caressing my butt cheeks.

"This feels so good," I moan.

"Aren't you forgetting something?" Aiden asks, pulling his hands from my body for a moment.

"What?"

"This feels so good, *sir*," he instructs.

"Yes, sir," I whisper as my heart skips another beat and I smile. His fingers return to me and make their way inside of my core. My legs spread over the arm chair to make extra room and he thrusts himself deep inside of me. My pleasure, mixed with a little pain, is completely intoxicating. I feel my body starting to pulsate.

"Ellie, you trust me, right?" Aiden asks.

"Yes, sir," I moan.

"This is going to be something new, but I think you'll enjoy it."

CHAPTER 19 - ELLIE

I look back. He gives me a big wet kiss and then pulls out a soft plastic thing, which starts out really narrow and then increases in width. It looks a little bit like a dildo, but not quite.

"Open your mouth," he says. I do as he says and he pushes it inside, letting me lick it. It's shorter than a dildo and quite narrow at the tip. It also has a little round part at the end where he holds it, as if it were a knob.

"What is it?" I ask in between my licks.

"It's a butt plug," he whispers in my ear. As I continue to suck on it, Aiden buries his fingers deep within and then spreads my wetness upward. He runs his fingers over my ass, and much to my surprise, it opens up for him. The feeling of his fingers inside of my butt feels a bit different. It's rougher and more primal and I get even more turned on.

"Oh, you like this, do you?" he asks.

"Yes, sir." I nod. "Very much."

Aiden pulls the butt plug from my mouth and slowly inserts it into my butt. As soon as the tip touches me, I suddenly reach the brink of orgasm. My body starts to move on its own, with my hips begging for more.

"Oh, Ellie, you're the hottest thing I've ever seen," he says. I moan in pleasure as he thrusts deeper and deeper within me. Without stopping, he gets up and moves around toward me. I grab onto his hard erect cock and lick it as hard as I can.

Aiden moans in pleasure and I moan along with him. I've never felt so full before, so full of pleasure.

"Oh, Aiden, I'm going to come," I whisper.

"No, you're not." He slows down his movements and I immediately regret bringing it up.

"No, don't stop," I say. "Don't ever stop."

"That's a good girl," he says and presses the butt plug deeper within me. At this point, my pleasure mixes with pain and I scream out. It goes so deep within me that it feels like every part of me is blocked, but in a delicious and very sexy way.

He pulls his hands away from my ass and toward my face. I continue to lick him, pushing him further and further down my throat. Slowly, he unties my hands and lets the scarf fall to the floor. Then he pulls away from me.

"Stay there," he instructs. I stay put as he walks over to the bed and lies down on his back with his hands behind his back.

"Okay, come over. Slowly. On your knees."

My heart skips a beat. I love how commanding he is; the control that I'm giving him. I also love how stimulated I feel despite the fact that he is across the room.

Slowly, I get down on my knees and come over to him on all fours. The plug in my butt moves along with each movement, and I feel like I'm going to come a few times on my way over.

Once I'm close enough, he pulls me up to my feet and on top of him. Slowly, he pushes himself deep inside of me and I moan in pleasure.

"Okay, come for me," he whispers. I press my lips onto his and lose myself completely. The orgasm rolls through me like a crashing wave. It builds and swells and spreads through me in a warm, overwhelming pulsation of pleasure.

Aiden threads his fingers in between mine as he comes as well. He pushes deeper and deeper in me until every part of me is filled with him. I moan and shift my body to accommodate the surges and rushes of his penis.

Aiden's loud breathing produces gusts along my throat and neck. I've lost all feeling in my legs, but I still manage to wrap them firmer around his hips. I want him even deeper inside of me.

"You're mine, you're all mine," Aiden moans, tossing his hair back.

Our hands are linked together and our bodies

become one. He tilts my mouth more toward his and kisses me hard and powerfully. He continues to glide in and out of me, but the tempo is slower now, less intense. With each movement, he stimulates the plug that's clenched in between my butt cheeks, and I start to feel another wave of orgasm start to build within me. I feel every rock-hard inch of him, and it feels like every inch of me belongs to him. I pull away to get some air, but he quickly pulls me in closer. His hands run all over my body and push my exposed breasts into his mouth as I thrash helplessly beneath him.

"You're so beautiful," Aiden says over and over. "You are my goddess."

I want to respond, but all I can manage is a moan in return.

When I finally do find the right words, "don't stop," is all I manage. We continue our delicate dance for some time and I feel him grow harder inside of me.

"How are you still doing this?" I whisper into his ear.

"Because you're so hot," he moans. His pace quickens and he runs his fingers down the small of my back and toward my ass. Then I feel him press on the plug.

"Oh my God," I moan from pleasure as he moves it around a little more, sending me to the heights of ecstasy. He is gentle but firm and steady and I can't handle it anymore.

"Aiden!" I cry out as a wave of pleasure cascades through my body. This time after the waves surge through me, my whole body goes numb and I collapse on top of him right there and then. I'm completely empty. Replete. Nothing else exists in the world except our sweaty bodies on this bed right here.

"I love you," Aiden whispers.

I think I say it back to him, but I don't really know.

"I want you to be mine," he says, pushing my hair out of my face and giving me a slight peck on my neck.

"I am yours," I manage, inhaling deeply.

"Forever."

I smile and close my eyes.

CHAPTER 20 - ELLIE

AFTERWARD…

I fall asleep again, completely spent after the intensity of our lovemaking. But I don't sleep for long. When I wake up, I glance at the clock. It has only been half an hour. I guess it was just a quick power nap. When I turn around, Aiden looks up at me from his phone and smiles.

"I love you," he whispers.

"I love you, too."

"What's new?" I ask, propping my head up with my hand. He shakes his head and runs his fingers over the outline of my face.

"Nothing." He shakes his head. "Nothing important at all.

We both know that he's lying, of course. Whatever emails he's getting now do not come with any good news. But I don't really want to talk or hear about it now. And he's clearly not in the mood for sharing either. Not yet. Not after the glorious thing that we have just gone through.

"Thank you," I say after a moment.

"For what?"

"For what you just did. For this whole night. It was amazing."

"You liked it?"

"I loved it," I say, nodding. "I've never done anything like that before and...it was so incredible."

"I'm glad."

"How did you know that I would like it?"

"I didn't. But I've seen how you responded to that kind of stimulation before...so, I thought I would give it a try."

I smile, sitting up. My lips are chapped and my throat is parched. There's a bottle of water on the end table and I open it, gulping all of it down.

"Oh, I'm sorry, did you want any?" I ask when it's already too late.

"No." Aiden laughs. "I have my own."

We sit on the bed in silence for a while. It occurs to me just how much I love being with Aiden. Just being with him. We don't have to talk or fill the silence with endless chatter. No, I just need him to be present.

Suddenly, Aiden hops out of bed and goes to his suitcase at the far end of the room. He's nude and I admire the way his muscles tense and clench as he glides through space.

"You are very sexy," I say. "Have I ever told you that?"

"Maybe once or twice," he says without turning around. "Okay, close your eyes."

"What?"

"Close your eyes. I have a surprise for you."

"If this is more sex, then I have to tell you, I need

a break."

"Just close your eyes, woman," Aiden says. Against my better judgment, I do as I'm told. Perhaps, there is some way he could get me into the mood again, but it would take a lot. And I'm already quite sore.

"Ellie," he says, taking my hand. I open my eyes and see him kneeling before me in all of his glory. He is on one knee. The faint light, the softness of candlelight, bathes his body and makes him look even more delicious and beautiful than I ever thought possible.

"Yes," I say, pulling the sheet around my chest. Despite how gorgeous he looks, the serious expression on his face gives me some concern. What's going on? What is he doing?

"Ellie, I have loved you since the first time I saw you. And ever since that moment, my love for you has just gotten deeper and deeper."

"I love you, too," I whisper.

"Whenever you're not around, all I can do is think about you. I crave you. I have to have you. I need you. You make me want to be a better man, Ellie."

Aiden pulls his right hand from behind his back and opens his palm. Tears well up in my eyes.

"What is this?" I whisper as I wipe them away and touch the outside of the little black velvet box in his hand.

"Ellie Rhodes," Aiden says, taking a deep breath. He lets go of my hand and puts it on top of the box. "My dearest, Ellie Rhodes. Will you marry me?"

I look at the ring inside the box. All I can make out through my tears is the band that's covered in a million tiny glittering crystals and the big yellow rock in the middle.

Aiden leans over to me and wipes my tears. When I look up at him, more tears stream down. All of my emotions are beyond my control at this point. This is the last thing I've expected him to ask me, and yet here we are.

"Will you marry me?" Aiden asks.

Before I can even think about it, my body responds for me.

"Yes, yes!" I exclaim and throw my arms around his neck. "I will marry you, Aiden Black."

CHAPTER 21 - AIDEN

WHEN I DECIDED TO ASK HER TO MARRY ME...

*W*hen I first met Ellie, I thought it was just infatuation. She is so beautiful that she took my breath away. And then I got to know her. Her kind heart and witty sense of humor surprised me at every turn. But still, never in a million years did I think that I would be ready to ask her to marry me.

The thing is that I do not have the best opinions about marriage. I see it as an old-fashioned institution that's in place to keep people in their place. Instead of being free agents, individuals, we are forced into being couples, or family groups. To share every part of ourselves, even down to our names. Of course, sharing a name isn't compulsory, but still, there's the expectation.

These are all the things that I've hated about marriage. But mostly, I hated the idea of being with just one person forever. But then I met Ellie. And now, somehow, everything that I was afraid of, everything that I dreaded, everything that I raged against, became insignificant. Instead of hating the idea of waking up with the same woman every morning, I look forward to it. Instead of worrying that I will get bored with her in a year, or five, or even within the month, I know that I won't and I look forward to starting the adventure of a lifetime.

Despite my reservations about marriage and love everlasting, I bought Ellie's engagement ring a week after I met her. It had rained all night and I tossed and turned and couldn't get a wink of shut-eye. In the morning, I decided to go on a run to clear my head. It wasn't even seven o'clock when I ran past a small boutique jewelry store, down an unfamiliar alleyway that I'd never gone down before. Most of the stores are still closed at this hour, but there was an old man shuffling around in the front, cleaning the windows. And that's when I saw it.

The ring had somewhat of an antique design with a glittering oval yellow gemstone at the center, surrounded by shiny bright stones all around and all the way down the band. I was going to just keep going, but I couldn't. It's as if it had stopped me and pulled me inside. I knocked on the door, but the old man waved me off.

"We're not open yet," he said.

"I know, I'm sorry," I yelled so he could hear me through the glass. "But if you could show me that ring there, I'd be really grateful."

The old man's face told me that he was nowhere near being convinced, but against his better judgement, he opened the front door.

"Which one?" he asked, grumpily.

"The one with the yellow stone," I said.

"It's a two-carat yellow diamond," he says, handing me the ring. "Are you going to propose?"

His salesmanship left much to be desired, but I liked him anyway. He wasn't a people-pleaser and that was a refreshing alternative to most people I dealt with on a daily basis.

"I don't know. I just met her," I said, picking up the ring and looking at it closer. Even though it was dark in the store and the clouds outside hung low and looming, this ring still sparkled as if it could make its own light.

"It's beautiful," I said.

"Yes, I know. It's one of my favorites."

"And these are all diamonds around the band?"

"Of course. High quality ones too."

I nodded, admiring the ring on my finger.

"Tell me about this girl."

"What do you mean?" I ask, taken a little aback.

"Well, this is my favorite ring. I bought this ring from a lonely old lady with no family or friends, but lots of money, who wanted it to go to a good home. She asked me what my dream was and I told her that my dream was to open a jewelry store. She gave me money to open this store, right here, and asked me to display this ring in the front. It was one of her favorites. She also asked me to sell it only to the right person."

"Oh wow," I mumble.

"Yes," the old man nodded. "And so far, in forty-seven years, I have not encountered such a person."

I smiled. Perhaps, this ring is not to be after all.

"So, tell me about this girl."

I took a deep breath. For a moment, I thought about lying about how we met because a man of his age probably wouldn't approve of our unconventional meeting place. But then, at the last minute, I decided against it. I was probably not going to get this ring anyway, so why lie?

I told him the truth. I told him about the yacht and the auction. I told him how I always assumed that I would be a bachelor for life, that I was simply incapable of loving one person forever.

"And you've only known her for a week?" the old man asked after listening very carefully.

Again, I was tempted to lie or at least obfuscate the truth. It sounded so sappy and stupid that I would feel this way about someone after such a short period of time. But again, I decided to go against my better judgement.

"Maybe that's not enough time, but it's just how I feel," I finally said. "I don't know much about her, of course, but every part of my being feels at home with her. I feel like I belong with her."

The man listened very carefully, and looked away after a few moments. I was sure that I had blown it. But I was glad that I told him the truth, even if I didn't deserve the ring. I had finally admitted something out loud that I had been terrified to admit to myself. I had admitted it and I was a better person for it.

"Well, thank you for your time," I said after a few moments. "You have a very beautiful ring, but I will not take up any more of your time."

I turned to leave, when the old man said, "And where do you think you're going?"

"What do you mean?"

"Do you want the ring or don't you?"

"You're really going to sell it to me?" I asked, not quite believing my ears.

"That is if you can afford it. It's not cheap."

"I didn't think it was."

The old man looked me up and down and then named the price. Fifty-eight thousand dollars. I nodded. It definitely wasn't cheap. But I just pulled out my credit card and handed it to him.

"So, what made you sell this ring to me after all of this time?" I asked, signing the receipt.

The old man looked up at me with tears in his eyes. "When you were telling me about Ellie, it reminded me a lot of how I felt about my Althea when we first met. I laid my eyes on her and I knew almost immediately. I did wait a week to ask her to marry me and then it took another month for her to agree. But once we got married, we were very happy for thirty-five glorious years. Until she passed away."

My heart tightened up at the thought. It both went out to him for all the pain that he went through and for myself, at the thought of losing Ellie.

"I'm so sorry about your loss," I whispered.

"Life happens," the old man shrugged. "But no matter how much it hurts now, I know that we were very happy when we were together and that nothing can take that away."

The old man packed the ring into a velvet ring box and handed it to me.

"Thank you very much," I said, and turned to leave.

"Oh, young man," he said, stopping me at the door. "Since you are now the owner of this very special ring, I thought you should know a little bit more about it."

I nodded.

"It was designed by a man named Captain Ludlow in England in 1860, for his beloved fiancé. She was sick with tuberculosis, and unfortunately it wasn't finished before she passed away. After her death, Captain Ludlow took the ring with him as he sailed around the world. It had been with him in South Africa, Argentina, Tahiti, China, San Francisco, and all around the Caribbean and the Mediterranean.

Captain Ludlow never married again, but instead held onto the ring as if it were his beloved's heart. He had it in his pocket when his ship went down off the coast of Veracruz, Mexico and he was rescued after surviving three long days and nights alone at sea, on a piece of wood. He had it when he was attacked by pirates off the coast of Algeria. Captain Ludlow continued to sail well into his eighties and he came to believe that the ring protected him from the many dangers he encountered.

He finally died from pneumonia doing what he loved best, sailing around the South Pacific. On his deathbed, he bequeathed the ring to his grand-niece, Ms. Elizabeth Ludlow, who later sold it to me and helped me to achieve my own dream. So, you see, Mr. Black, this is a very special ring. It will not only protect you in times of peril and turmoil, but also give you hope when all feels lost. I hope you treat it well."

CHAPTER 22 - ELLIE

$\mathcal{W}$e got back from Maine a couple of days ago. Aiden spent the night last night and has been gone all day, busy with work stuff. Caroline is out of the hospital and spending a lot of time alone in her room. I check on her every few hours, bring her food and tea, but she isn't very interested. According to the hospital staff, she's all better, physically. But the emotional toll of what happened in Maine will take a lot to recover from. I want her to see a psychologist or a therapist, but I haven't gotten the courage to bring it up quite yet. She's not even ready to leave her room yet. I doubt that she has the energy to go talk to anyone. Luckily, there was a psychiatrist at the hospital who prescribed her some medication to calm her down. That should tide her over for some time.

I sit at my desk, looking at the gloomy late fall weather outside. Thanksgiving is over and Christmas isn't for another month. Holiday decorations are popping up all over town, brightening the mood that the gray weather has put a damper onto. As I stare at the open document in front of me, with barely a paragraph written on my new book, my gaze drops down to my fingers. There it is. Wow.

My heart skips a beat.

It's still hard to believe that this perfect canary yellow diamond ring is a symbol of my engagement to the most amazing man in the world. I love the antique style of the ring and it must've cost him a fortune, but I would've loved it even if it were sterling silver and a cubic zirconia. I would've loved it even if it were a ring pop. I know that now. I would've loved it no matter what, because it was given to me by Aiden Black, the man who stole my heart.

A tear forms at the corner of my eye and I gasp for

air. I still can't believe that this is happening. A proposal was the last thing that I expected. I knew that we were in love, but I had no idea that he was ready for such a commitment. Frankly, I didn't think I was either until I said yes. His proposal caught me off guard, but not as much as my own reply. And yet, at the same time, it felt like the most normal and natural thing in the world. The word 'yes' loomed in my mind even before he finished asking me. I almost didn't have the patience to wait until he was done.

Okay, enough with all of this, I say to myself. I check my emails to distract myself. There are about twenty from my readers. They are in love with my book and can't wait for the next installment. This warms my heart. Not many readers know this, but one of the main reasons we, writers, write is for this moment. Writing is a very solitary endeavor where you spend a lot of time alone in your room with your nose buried in the computer screen. But then, once the book comes out, all bets are off. Even the most experienced and famous writers will tell you that (if they dare to admit it to themselves) there's nothing like hearing from a reader about how much your book has impacted their life.

When I first started, I promised myself that I would

reply to each and every one of the emails. My readers took the time to write and I will take a few moments to show them my appreciation. After replying to the first seven emails in my inbox, I open the eighth. This one is different. This one doesn't just say how much she loved my book even though it does say that.

I LOVED YOUR BOOK. I loved the premise and your writing. It really took me away to another world and for that I'm forever thankful. My husband, the love of my life, was recently diagnosed with cancer and I've been spending a lot of time with him in the hospital. As you probably know, hospitals are dreary places especially if you're there helping the love of your life fight for his. And so, the reason why I'm reaching out is that I want to thank you. From the bottom of my heart. Your book took me away to another world and helped me forget about my own life, if only for a brief period of time. It's an escape that I won't soon forget and I can't wait for the next book.

TEARS ARE RUNNING down my face when I finish reading her email. I never knew that my writing could make such an impact on someone's life, and for her to share this with me, makes my heart swell. I want to wrap my arms around her and tell her that it's all going to be okay. But of course, I can't. No, I need to express my feelings in words, which isn't always an easy thing.

For a moment, I think about putting this task to the side and doing it sometime later, but as more tears stream down my cheeks, I know that I can't.

I'M sorry to hear about your husband's diagnosis. I wish there were something I could do. You are a very strong woman and going through this will make you even stronger. I am thinking about you and your husband and hope that everything turns out okay.

You have no idea how much your email means to me. I write partly because I have to for myself and partly for my readers. I love hearing how much you enjoyed my book, but I had no idea that it would help you so much in your time of need. I am truly humbled. I will get back to work ASAP to give you more enjoyment and a moment of escape. Again, my thoughts are with you and your husband and please keep me updated about his treatment.

.   .   .

AFTER I FINISH THE EMAIL, my head is not in a good place to produce fiction (or even mostly autobiographical fiction). I close my computer and say a silent thank you. Even though my life is full of its own struggles, I can't imagine going through something like this.

***

WHEN I COME out to the living room, I find Caroline on the couch, flipping through the channels. She's dressed in pajamas, thick socks, and a bathrobe. Her hair is a total mess, unwashed for many days, and she isn't wearing a spot of makeup. If you know anything about Caroline like I do, you know that she isn't one to even exit her room without a full face of makeup in the morning. Despite this, I decide to take her presence in the living room as a good sign.

"Can I watch with you?" I ask. She shrugs. I watch her flip on HGTV, then on local news, CNN, and then back to HGTV. Finally, she seems to settle on a show about a couple looking to buy a house in Costa Rica.

"Is this place really real?" Caroline asks absentmindedly.

"Apparently," I say. I know exactly what she means. The color of the water that appears on the screen seems unreal, just as unreal as the palm trees gently swaying in the breeze.

"Maybe we can go there sometime," I say. "Just you and me."

She pauses for a moment, as if she's actually considering the proposition. "Yeah, maybe," she says after a moment. I want to believe her, but I know that she's just placating me. Still, I choose to believe that one day, when all of this blows over, it will be possible.

We watch one episode and then another and another. I keep wanting to bring up what happened in Maine or what is going on with the investigation now, but I can't summon the strength. Every time I look over at Caroline, the only thing I can think of is the phrase 'shell-shocked.' It's a term used to describe soldiers returning from World War I, before we got more sophisticated phrases like 'post-traumatic stress disorder.' I know that this is what she's going through, yet the phrase 'shell-shocked' seems much more appropriate than PTSD, at this point. Caroline looks lost. Buried somewhere deep within herself. I know that it hasn't been very long since we got back from Maine. I know that I need to give her time to recover. But I'm impatient. I want my friend back. I want to see her smiling face. Her carefree demeanor. I want to hear her witty comments. And, more than anything, I'm terrified that if I let her disappear into herself like this for any length of time, I will lose her forever.

CHAPTER 23 - ELLIE

WHEN THEY FIND OUT…

a few hours later, I get a text. Aiden is downstairs and I buzz him in. I meet him at the front door and he gives me a big kiss on the lips. It sends shivers down my spine and I revel in the total feeling of adoration and love. When we finally pull away from one another, I catch a glance of us in the hallway mirror. He has his strong arms wrapped tightly around my shoulders. His eyes are cast down a bit and a few strands of hair fall in his face. He licks his lips and flashes me a smile.

"What ya staring at, beautiful?"

"You."

Aiden tilts my body back and runs his fingers down my neck and over the top of my breasts as he kisses me behind the ear.

A few moments later, I suddenly catch myself and pull away from him.

"What's wrong?"

"No, nothing," I say. That's not entirely true. "Well, the thing is that Caroline's in her room. And I don't want her to come out and see us..."

I don't really know why I don't want her to see us. But Aiden fills in the blank.

"Yes, that would be difficult for her."

I smile at him. We have not known each other for very long and yet he already knows what I'm thinking. Is this really happening?

"So, shall we?" Aiden asks, taking me by the hand. I squeeze it and follow him into the living room.

No fancy night out tonight. No high heels or short black dresses. No suit for Aiden.

"We have quite a glamorous affair planned for

tonight, don't we?" I ask, as I open the drawer with all the takeout menus.

Aiden laughs as he plops himself in front of the television.

"An evening spent in our pajamas, vegetating on the couch?"

"Vegetating?" he asks.

"You know, like Cher from Clueless called it? Being still like vegetables." I say.

"Wow, now that's a blast from the past."

We order some Thai food from my favorite place around the corner and flip on Netflix to try to find the perfect complement to their amazing stir fry ginger dish and yellow curry. Ten minutes later, when the food arrives, Aiden and I fight over who is going to cover the bill. Finally, he gives in. I recognize that this is a small victory, but I'm glad to take whatever I can get.

"Caroline?" I knock on her door. "We got a lot of Thai food. Do you want to come out and have some?"

I don't hear a response for a few moments. "No thanks," she says after a while through the door.

"Can I bring you some in there then? You haven't had much to eat today."

"No thanks."

I look back at Aiden who just shrugs his shoulders and digs in. He knows that there isn't much we can do to make her eat or feel better unless she lets us. But I have a much harder time accepting this fact.

"Okay, fine," I finally give in and plop onto the couch next to Aiden. He picks some crime thriller on Netflix and I agree to watch it because my mind is elsewhere. I'm really worried about Caroline and I hate feeling this helpless. Whenever there's a problem I like to take the initiative. I'm not someone who wallows for long. But then again, I've never been through anything like Caroline experienced.

"She just needs time," Aiden says. "It's going to take a bit for her to process everything."

"Yes, I know. You're right. Of course, you're right."

As Aiden turns his attention to his fried wontons

and the movie, I pull out my phone. My mind is going a mile a minute and somehow scrolling through meaningless stuff online makes it slow down. Maybe not slow down exactly, but at least distract me somewhat.

My guilty pleasure is the juicy gossip sites about celebrities. I hate to admit it, but I love looking at the pictures of the pregnancy and birth announcements. I love reading about how so and so lost twenty pounds and who is dating who now. I'm not proud of it, but that's why it's a guilty pleasure, right?

"Oh my God," I say, nearly dropping my phone. The image that pops up onto the screen makes me jump out of my seat. I look closer to make sure that my eyes aren't deceiving me.

"This can't be real," I mumble.

Aiden is too engrossed in the action on screen to pay much attention to me.

"Aiden," I say slowly. "Look."

It takes him a few moments to pull himself away from the television.

"What?" he asks, absentmindedly.

I hand him the phone. He looks at the screen and then at me. And then back to the screen.

"What is this?"

"The Daily Dish," I say.

"No, I mean, why are there pictures of us here?"

"I don't know," I whisper.

But it's as clear as day, there are two pictures of us. In the first, we are walking hand in hand together from a restaurant. By the outfit, I know that it was taken before we went to Maine. And in the second, Aiden is kissing me under a tree.

"Is this one from the party?" Aiden asks.

"Yes, I think so."

"So, someone at the Warrenhouse party took a picture of us and sold it to this trash mag?"

It definitely looks like it. But why? I mean, who the hell am I to be in a gossip magazine? And even Aiden? I mean, he runs a big company, but he isn't a celebrity. At least, not in any real way. Right?

"I don't understand why we're here at all. I mean, who cares?"

"Well, with my business blowing up in a very public way, I guess people are much more interested in me than they used to be."

Of course. Man, am I an idiot. I completely forgot. Aiden Black is a public figure. And even though he was never really in that many gossip magazines before, except maybe on Page Six, when he was seen with a particular socialite, now that Owl is in trouble, there's much more fodder for gossip.

Before I even have a few minutes to process any of this, my phone lights up. It's my mom. I press ignore and turn off my phone. A voicemail appears a minute later. It's then quickly followed by a succession of texts.

WHERE ARE YOU?

I just saw your picture in the Daily Dish.

YOU'RE SEEING AIDEN BLACK?

.   .   .

WHY DIDN'T you tell me?

ELLIE, answer the phone!

SHIT, I had forgotten that I got my love for gossip magazines from none other than my own mother.

"Who is that?" Aiden asks.

"My mom. She saw the article too."

"Answer it," he says, absentmindedly.

"The thing is that I never told her about us," I say. My mouth can't keep up with my thoughts as I start to slur my words in an effort to get everything out at once. "Not yet. I mean, you asked me to marry you so suddenly and now it seems like a big secret, but it's really not."

Aiden shrugs. "It's no big deal. I didn't tell anyone either."

"So, what should I do now?"

"I guess, you should tell her that you are seeing me. I mean, what's the point of lying now?"

"You're right. Of course, you're right," I nod.

I take a deep breath and pick up the phone. "Mom?"

***

To say that my mom is freaking out over seeing my picture in the Daily Dish would be the understatement of a lifetime. She is over the moon. She wants to know all the details. Where did I meet Aiden? How long have we been together? What is he like? And, most importantly, why didn't I tell her?

I don't really have any good answers to any of this, so I decide to be as vague as possible. We met at a party that Caroline invited me to. It was on a yacht, but I don't mention the auction. He's wonderful, of course, but I don't mention that we are engaged quite yet. That can wait until we meet in person. Why didn't I tell her? Because I wasn't sure where it was going and I wasn't ready to talk about it quite yet.

"Well, you absolutely have to invite him over for

dinner," Mom says after listening very carefully. "We must meet him as soon as possible."

"Mom..." I start to say.

"Don't Mom me," she says sternly. "You kept the biggest story of the year from me and I had to find out about you dating a billionaire in an online magazine!"

"I'm not sure about it being the biggest story of the year."

"It is for me!"

"Okay, I'll give you that," I say.

"So, I can give you a choice of dates. This Wednesday or Thursday."

"Wednesday is tomorrow!" I protest.

"And Thursday is the day after. I'm glad that Ivy League education is finally paying off."

She can't see me, but I'm rolling my eyes.

"Okay, hold on," I say, putting my hand over the bottom of the phone.

"My mom wants us to come over for dinner," I

whisper. "Tomorrow or the day after. I can try to postpone it until next week, but that will probably be it."

Aiden looks up at me. "Tomorrow is fine," he says with a shrug.

"Really?"

"Yeah, why not? I'd love to meet your parents."

CHAPTER 24 - ELLIE

WHEN WE GO TO CONNECTICUT...

*A*fter eating takeout and watching Netflix on the couch, I want Aiden to spend the night, but he has an early meeting the following day so he goes back home to his apartment. He has an important meeting with the shareholders tomorrow morning and has to be in fighting spirits.

The following day, I spend writing, answering emails, trying to get Caroline to leave her room, and deciding what to wear. I don't want to be too dressed up because then Mom will immediately know what's up. But at the same time, I can't very well just show up in a pair of pajamas. Aiden will be picking me up straight from work, so he will be wearing an expensive suit and looking quite dashing like always.

What about a pair of skinny jeans and heels and a blazer? Jeans would say it's a casual evening, but the heels would go well with Aiden's outfit and not make me look too out of place. Shit, this is exactly what I need Caroline around for. Clothes are her specialty, not mine. But when I knock on her door and ask her for help, she just says she's tired.

I wash my hair and put on my makeup. I look at myself in the mirror and my heart skips a beat. Tonight, everything is going to become real. My mom will know that I'm engaged. It's not like the engagement didn't feel real before this moment, but there's nothing like those people who are closest to you sharing in your joy. At least, that's what all the movies say, right?

Okay, okay, calm down, I say to myself. Mom is going to be very excited and somebody has to remain calm in this type of situation. I pull on the skinny jeans and wedges. These are really summer shoes, the old Caroline would point out, but I love that they have the toes covered. My feet always get really cold walking the New York streets in early December. Plus, wedges are much easier to walk in than regular stilettos or even high heels.

My phone lights up. It's a text from Aiden.

I'M DOWNSTAIRS.

"CAROLINE, I'm leaving. See you later," I yell. I wait for a moment in the hallway as I put on my jacket, but she doesn't respond.

***

"Hey!" I climb into Aiden's car and give him a kiss on the lips. "Man, it's cold out there." ***

"Yeah, I know," he mumbles and pulls away from the curb.

"You know the address?"

"Nope," he says.

Something about his one line responses feels odd. We drive for a while without saying a word. This is unusual, but I try not to pay too much attention to it. Not yet, anyway.

"I'm really nervous about your meeting Mom and Mitch," I say. I want to develop some sort of strategy in how to deal with everything at their house. Maybe even a code. But we don't have much time. And, from the looks of it, Aiden doesn't seem to be in the mood.

"Why is that?" he asks.

"Well, you know, it's not every day that I bring a fiancé over to their house," I say jokingly. I expect him to flash a knowing smile. Or at least, chuckle a little bit. But instead, I get nothing.

"Are you okay?" I ask after a moment of silence. "Is something wrong?"

"No, not really," he says with a shrug. Then he leans over and turns up the music.

Annoyed, I shake my head. I give out an audible sigh to get his attention. But it's all to no avail. I lean over and turn down the music.

"Aiden?"

"What?" he asks, without taking his eyes off the road.

"What's going on? Do you not want to do this?"

"Of course, I do."

"So, why do things feel so...off?"

He doesn't say anything for a moment. "I don't know."

I continue to press the situation, but unfortunately I don't get any further with this line of questioning. We listen to music the rest of the drive over. It is one of the longest forty minutes of my life.

When we finally arrive at Mom and Mitch's house in Greenwich, Connecticut, I'm regretting the whole night, but it's too late to go back. Mom will be furious if I were to cancel and I know that she probably went all out for dinner. No matter how much money they have, she rarely caters or hires a chef. Cooking is one of her favorite things to do in the world.

"Aiden, you have to talk to me. We're going in there to meet my parents. You can't be so closed off," I say. "If you don't want to be here then tell me. I can do this myself."

"No, let's just get this over with," he mumbles as he

pulls into the driveway. I shake my head. This is not going to go well, I know it already. But I'm at a loss as to what to do.

Aiden gets out of the car first and waits for me to walk to the door. He doesn't make one comment about how beautiful the house looks with all the Christmas lights outside. I, on the other hand, find them breathtaking. The house that I grew up in from the age of eleven looks like it belongs in the pages of *Connecticut Life* or *Town and Country* magazine. Perfect white lights illuminate and frame the gables, window and the front door. I see my mom standing in the foyer even before we get to the steps.

"Mom!" I yell and wrap my arms around her neck. She gives me a warm hug in return. "It's so nice to see you."

Mom is dressed in an elegant short black dress, black tights and stilettos. She is petite with short blonde hair that falls into her face, framing it just so. Her diamond stud earrings shine brightly and her tiny waist is accentuated by the white and red apron wrapped tightly around it.

"You look beautiful," I say. "As always."

Mom pulls away from me and looks me up and down. "As do you."

"Mom, I'd like you to meet Aiden."

"Yes, of course," Mom says, extending her hand to him. Aiden is standing slightly behind me and takes a moment to approach her and come into the light. I hate that she is meeting him on such a sour occasion. I hate that he isn't his usual charming self, but there isn't much I can do about it.

"It's a pleasure to meet you, Mrs. Rhodes."

"Oh please, call me Margie," Mom says, laughing and throwing her head back. "And I haven't been Mrs. Rhodes for a long time."

When she closes the door behind us and hangs my coat in the closet, I see Mitch come downstairs. He's dressed in an elegant suit and his thick dark hair is only now getting a few sprinkles of salt and pepper in it. Even though it has been years, he's as handsome as he was when Mom married him.

After giving me a warm hug, I introduce Aiden and he and Mitch shake hands.

"It's a pleasure to meet you, Aiden. I've heard a lot about you."

"All good, I hope," Aiden jokes. I'm surprised that he says this and hope that perhaps he can fake some pleasantries long enough to get through dinner.

"Yes, of course."

"The house looks amazing," I say, looking around at all the expert Christmas decor around their six-bedroom, six bath home with a two-bedroom pool house out back. "It's like you're living in a Pottery Barn catalog."

"Close," Mitch laughs. "But a tad more expensive. Try West Elm."

"Oh c'mon," Mom laughs. "You said you liked how it looked."

"And I do. But I didn't enjoy getting the credit card bill for this little project, let me tell you, Ellie," Mitch says.

I smile and give Mitch a brief squeeze. This is how they have been since they've met. They banter and complain about each other and they also love each other to pieces. Never for a moment did I ever doubt that Mom and Mitch belong together, unlike Mom and Dad. I hate to admit it, but my mom and dad were never a good fit. When they argued, they were mean-spirited and when they weren't fighting, things weren't much better. Even back then, when I was quite little, I knew that my parents weren't meant to be together and I made a promise to myself that I would never be in a relationship like that.

CHAPTER 25 - AIDEN

I knew that it was a mistake to come here even before I even picked up Ellie. It would've been selfish to cancel, but it's more selfish to go despite the fact that I'm not in the right headspace to meet my fiancée's parents. Fiancée. At this point, that word doesn't even make sense anymore. I mean, who the hell am I to marry this beautiful woman? Can I even make her happy? Definitely not as long as I'm in the state that I'm in. And how long will this last? Likely a very long time.

They fired me.

I showed up to the meeting with the Board of Directors to try to figure out a way to make all of this work and they just fucking fired me. It didn't matter that I started the company. It didn't matter that I was the CEO. None of that mattered. The shareholders are unhappy with the direction that Owl is going in, so they just got rid of me.

I knew they were unhappy, but I never knew they were capable of anything like this. I mean, who the hell do they think they are? Did they invest their blood, sweat and tears into this? No, they're just a bunch of old rich assholes who don't know their elbows from their assholes. And yet, they have the power to fire me at will and hire some dick who probably never even heard of Owl before to run it.

My blood boils at the thought of that, and yet here we are. Thanks to Blake, all major investors pulled out and that's somehow my fault. If only they knew the truth. If only they knew that Blake deserves to be in jail for what he did, and tried to do, to Ellie. But no, he's out there walking free and there are people who are actually listening to him about the direction that Owl should take.

"Aiden, are you listening?" Ellie whispers in my ear as her mom gives me a tour of their house.

"Yes, of course," I say quickly. My eyes meet Margie's

and when she launches into another aspect of the recent remodel that the house underwent, I nod quickly and ferociously to look as interested as I possibly can.

I know that this evening is going all wrong. I shouldn't be here. Hell, Ellie shouldn't be here. This is not how I wanted to meet her parents. What I should be doing is telling Ellie what happened today at work. But I can't think straight tonight. All I feel is anger boiling up from somewhere deep within me.

"Well, I think we're ready for dinner now," Margie says and I nod again. After handing me a glass of whiskey, Mitch disappears into the kitchen with Margie.

I follow Ellie into the living room, taking three big gulps of my drink. As the dark brown liquid runs down the back of my throat, I feel some of the stress lift from my shoulders.

"What the hell, Aiden?" Ellie whispers as she shows me to the dining room table.

"What?"

"It's like you're not here. Why did you even agree to come?"

"I'm sorry. I'm just going through some things at work."

I want to tell her the truth. More than anything. But I can't. Her parents will return any minute and then what? She will have more questions and I'm just not ready for this conversation. Not until I drown my sorrows in the whole bottle of whiskey.

When everyone is seated and Margie and Mitch bring out the food, we both oh and ah over how delicious it is. I make a great effort to appear as if everything is as normal as possible, but I'm having a hard time judging whether or not anyone is buying it.

"So, Aiden, I can't lie, I have of course heard of Owl and the great success that you made of that company," Mitch says. He works on Wall Street and not in some junior associate position either. I'm sure that Mitch Willoughby not only heard about Owl's success, but also its downfall.

"Well, thank you, sir," I say. "It has been quite a ride."

"Tell me, how did you get it started? I love to hear stories about entrepreneurship."

"Mitch is a big Shark Tank fan, in case you were wondering," Ellie adds. I smile.

"I was in college - Yale..."

"Oh! Ellie's and my alma mater!"

"Yes, Ellie told me that, sir," I say. "I was always into computers a lot. Didn't have many friends growing up. And the idea sort of came to me. It's not really that original, of course. It's just an online retailer like Amazon."

"Oh, you're just being modest," Mitch says. "There are, of course, a lot of online retailers. But very few of them are Amazon. Seriously, it's quite remarkable that you were able to grow it to the level at which it exists today. Amazon considers you to be their main threat. Even more so than Walmart. Of course, I'm sure you know that already."

I smile, nod, and finish my whiskey. He quickly pours me another - a man after my own heart. After I'm sufficiently lubricated, I feel a lot looser and not so standoffish. Suddenly, engaging in conversation doesn't require that much effort. Mitch and Margie continue to ask me about Owl and I actually reply in more than a few words.

"So, can you tell me of any big mergers or acquisitions that are coming up?" Mitch asks when we all finish our food.

"Oh c'mon, you and I both know that I can't talk about that," I say.

"We will just keep this between friends."

I shake my head. This is how investment bankers are. He's asking me to break the law. He's asking me to commit insider trading, but to him it barely registers as an offense.

"Your father wants insider information, Ellie," I say. "Do you know what that means?"

"Isn't that what Martha Stewart went to jail for?"

"No, that's what she went to prison for," I correct her.

CHAPTER 26 - AIDEN

WHEN THINGS GET A LITTLE TENSE...

*M*y joke about Martha Stewart puts a stop to Mitch's casual search for insider information. Normally, I'd continue with the easy-going banter so that Mitch would start to feel more comfortable with me. But today, I don't have the energy.

Luckily, Margie changes the subject.

"So, Ellie, how's your writing going?"

The expression on Ellie's face changes immediately.

"Um, fine," she mumbles and takes a few sips of wine. "Well, actually, really well. The readers are really responding well to my work."

"Now that's really exciting," Margie says.

"Yes, it's really refreshing."

"How so?" Mitch asks.

"Well, you know when I worked at Buzz Post, no one really cared about those stupid little quizzes that I wrote. I mean, people liked them, they brought in all the clicks, but no one reached out to me like they do now."

"Readers are loving her book," I pipe in. Finally, I can contribute something positive to the conversation and avoid talking about work, my own rather sad state of affairs. "You should see all the emails that she's getting."

Ellie smiles from ear to ear. "I never knew that I could have such an impact. Or that anyone would be affected enough to actually reach out to me. I mean, I myself, have read and enjoyed a lot of books, but I never really wrote the author and told them how I felt."

"Yes, I had no idea that anyone really did that," Margie says.

"Well, they do," Ellie says beaming. "At least my fans

do. And it's amazing. I mean, writing can be quite solitary work, so it's nice to get real feedback. And not just feedback, really good, kind words. My writing is actually helping some of my readers get through some very hard times in their lives. Providing an escape, you know?"

"Is that so?" Margie asks.

Ellie nods and gives me a smile. Despite everything that's going on with my own career, I'm really proud of her. Her dreams are finally coming true and it's a privilege to be here to experience it with her.

"I'm really happy for you," I say.

"Aiden has been very supportive," Ellie explains as if an explanation is necessary. But by the look on Margie's face, apparently, it is.

"Aren't you proud of your daughter?" I ask. "I know I am."

"Yes, of course," Margie says with not much enthusiasm. "But you know, of course, Mitch and I hope that she starts to write something more serious in the future."

"More serious?" I ask, glancing over at Ellie. The smile on her face vanishes in an instant.

"Well, you know. Romance?" Margie says with a smirk. "And self-publishing?"

"I don't understand," Ellie whispers.

"Oh c'mon, Ellie, please" Margie scoffs at her. "You know that you are capable of so much more than self-publishing so-called romance."

"Your daughter is very talented," I interrupt. I can't stand listening to this shit, but Ellie puts her hand on my knee under the table to calm me down.

"Yes, I know that. That's why I'm saying what I'm saying. We all know that she is very talented and this line of work just isn't suitable for someone like her. I mean, you went to Yale for crying out loud. You were on your way to becoming a serious journalist."

"I was not," Ellie says. "I was writing stupid little quizzes at some online magazine that gets advertising money through click bait articles."

"They do publish serious news as well."

"So what? That wasn't my job. Besides, I never

wanted to be a journalist. I always wanted to write fiction."

"And you're happy writing what you're writing?"

"And what am I writing, mother?" Ellie asks, crossing her arms across her chest.

"You know very well. But if you want me to come out and say it, then I guess I will."

"Why don't you?" she asks, squeezing my knee ever harder.

"Porn. You write porn, my darling," Margie says. "You and I know this very well. And so does anyone else who comes across your books."

"No, I don't write porn, mother. I write romance books with sex in them. I write romance the way it exists in the world. It doesn't just all fade to black you know, when people go to bed. I describe what happens between people because what happens in bed is important. And sexy. And relevant. My book has a sexually-empowered main character and I won't apologize for creating her. Not to you. And not to anyone else."

"You're impossible," Margie whispers, shaking her head. "Mitch talk to her."

"Margie, I think it's fine for Ellie to do what she wants to do. She seems to be enjoying her work, so why not?"

"Oh, c'mon, Mitch. Please. Give me a break. You think what she writes is smut and you told me so yourself. So, why the fuck are you giving us this cop out now?"

"Well, my darling," Mitch says. I'm starting to notice that their use of terms of endearment aren't exactly the same as other people's. "Because we have company here and perhaps this isn't the best time to talk about Ellie's career choices."

Margie shakes her head.

"Listen, mom, I'm going to make this really easy on you. We don't have to talk about this anymore. Aiden and I are going to go."

"What? No."

"Yes," Ellie says and gets up to leave.

"But we haven't had dessert yet."

"We're going to pass."

"Aiden," Margie reaches out to me. She puts her long cold fingers on my forearm, but I just brush her off.

"Your daughter is a very talented writer and I'm sorry for you that you don't understand that," I say. "Thank you for dinner."

"Ellie, I don't understand why you're getting so mad. I was just expressing my opinion."

"Well, your opinion...sucks. It really sucks, Mom. I don't know what I'm going to do in the future. I don't know what kind of books I'm going to write. But for right now, I'm really enjoying doing what I'm doing. I love the emails that I'm getting from my readers and when I shared that with you, you just pissed all over it. Why? Does it make you feel better to put me down?"

"I didn't mean to put you down. I just wanted you to know that you are capable of so much more."

It's hard to put into words the rage and hatred I feel for Margie at this very moment. I hate her passive aggressive bullshit and her backhanded compliment that's not a compliment at all. And most of all, I hate the pain that she is causing Ellie.

I'm about to say something, when Ellie breaks out in laughter. Then she shakes her head and rolls her eyes. "Fuck you, Mom. Okay? How about that? Why don't you just go fuck yourself?"

She takes me by the arm and pulls me toward the front door.

CHAPTER 27 - ELLIE

AFTER DINNER...

Well, that didn't go as well as I thought it would. Aiden gives me a brief hug as we leave their house, but I just push him away. I can't deal with physical contact right now. I'm fuming. My heart is racing and I need to get myself under control first.

"It's going to be okay," Aiden says. I nod in agreement, but I don't believe him. I want to scream at the top of my lungs and pound on something really hard. But instead, I let him lead me to his car. He opens the door and waits for me to get in. He gives me too much time. He hesitates for too long. Everything is compounding my anger. I reach out and close the door myself. I shut it right in his face, but he doesn't seem fazed by it.

When he gets into the car, he doesn't say anything else. He simply starts the engine and drives off. I let out a big sigh of relief. The heaviness of the world doesn't disappear off my shoulders, but it feels like someone is there holding up some of it for me.

Twenty minutes later, I'm finally ready to talk again.

"I'm really sorry about dinner," I say. "I shouldn't have made a scene like that."

"Your mom was really out of line."

"I know, but still. She's always like that. She isn't exactly the most supportive person when it comes to...anything."

"You don't say," he jokes.

"I don't really understand what her issue is. I mean, she's married to Mitch, they have a lot of money. Mitch will always provide for me if I let him. He's quite generous like that. So, why was she always so unhappy about me becoming a writer?"

"Even before you started writing romance?"

"Yes. She acts like BuzzPost is this ideal place for me to work, but you should've heard her comments about it when I started. 'You spent four years at Yale. Your education cost over two-hundred thousand dollars, and now you're writing online quizzes asking people what kind of wedding they should have based on their favorite Harry Potter house.'"

"I'm sorry," Aiden says.

I know that I'm overwhelming him with my problem when he clearly has enough of his own, but I can't help it. I'm fuming. Why does my mother have to be this way? Why can't she be happy for me? Doesn't she know how few people there are out there who get paid anything at all for their writing? And I have people buying my books? Who cares if the first book was only ninety-nine cents and my cut of it is only thirty-five cents. It's still something. She has no idea how hard it is for writers to get anyone to pay for their books.

"She just makes me so angry, Aiden. I mean, I have readers who are actually paying money to read my fiction. I mean, that's a miracle. Most people will pay three bucks for a cup of coffee at Starbucks every day and think nothing of it. But then they will also complain that a whole book, which takes a couple of months to write, costs more than ninety-nine cents. And yet, I have people buying my books. Not many people, but enough to make me feel like I'm doing something worthwhile."

"I'm really sorry, Ellie. I wish she was more supportive. Not sure if it matters, but I'm really proud of you."

"Thank you."

Of course it matters. His support means everything. And yet, it doesn't erase the bad taste in my mouth from my mom's reaction at dinner.

"I'm sorry. I shouldn't let this bother me so much," I say when we pull up to my apartment building. "She's always been this way. And it doesn't really matter in the grand scheme of things."

"Of course, it does," Aiden says. "But I understand what you mean."

We sit in silence for a bit, listening to Adele, who just came on the radio. Her song *Hello* makes for a good soundtrack for this evening.

"Would you like to come up?" I ask.

He shrugs.

"You don't?"

"No, it's not that. I do. But I have a lot on my mind," he says after a moment.

I nod and wait for him to continue. But he doesn't.

"So, you aren't going to come up?" I ask. He shrugs.

"Do you have something going on at work tomorrow?" I press.

He shrugs.

"Aiden, what's going on?"

"Nothing."

I feel like I'm pulling teeth. But this time he doesn't give in.

"C'mon, why don't you come up? We can have some tea and cookies? Go to bed?"

I need him to spend the night with me. How much more obvious do I have to be?

"Not tonight," he says after a moment.

"What's wrong?" I ask, refusing to let the subject go.

He hesitates for a bit, but when he realizes that I'm not going to let him off that easily, he finally caves.

"Something happened at work today," Aiden says. "Something bad."

"What?"

My head starts to buzz when he says the word 'fired.'

"But I don't understand…"

"I don't know what to tell you," Aiden shrugs. "I had a meeting with the board today and they let me go."

"But you're the founder of the company. How can they just fire you?"

"Because they're the board. They have more power than I do. If I stop making the shareholders money, then they can replace me with someone who will. It's business."

I shake my head.

"But you never even sexually harassed anyone or had any scandals. I thought that's what people got fired for."

"Well, actually, you are much less likely to get fired

for sexually harassing a woman than for not making money. Unfortunately."

I continue to pepper him with questions even as I can see that he is reluctant to answer them. But a few minutes later, he shuts down.

"Ellie, I'm sorry, but you have to get out of the car," he says. "I just can't talk about this anymore. And I know that if I come up that's all we're going to talk about."

He's right, of course. I know that. But it still hurts. Tears start to well up in the back of my throat. I'm not sure if I'm about to cry because of his job, my mom, or the fact that I didn't much sleep the night before.

I take a deep breath and open the door.

"I'll call you later," he says, grabbing my arm just as I'm about to exit. I give him a brief squeeze back and slam the door behind me. Once I disappear behind the safety of my building's front door, and I'm well out of earshot and eyesight of Aiden, I burst into tears.

I wipe my tears before entering my apartment. I don't want Caroline to see me distraught. She has enough to worry about for now. I like the idea of being there for her, and being her rock, but I'm not sure if I'm strong enough for anyone to break against right now. When I walk into the foyer, I expect to see the door to Caroline's room closed as it had been for days. When I see that it is, I head straight to my room.

"Hey," Caroline says from the couch.

"Oh hey. How are you?"

I want to climb under my covers and go to sleep forever. But Caroline hasn't been out and about under her own volition for a while. I know that I wouldn't be a good friend if I didn't take a few moments to acknowledge this momentous achievement.

"How are you?" I ask, heading to the refrigerator.

After staring absent-mindedly at the empty shelves, I pour myself a glass of water. I hope that I've wasted enough time that my eyes no longer look like they've recently seen tears.

"Okay," she shrugs. "I ordered some Chinese. Want some?"

Wow, she actually took the initiative to order takeout? She must be feeling a lot better.

"No thanks. I just got back from dinner."

"With Aiden?"

"And my parents."

"Wow, that must've been intense."

"Tell me about it," I say. And just like that, within practically a moment, things suddenly feel somewhat normal. It's almost as if Maine never happened.

"So..." Caroline says, changing the channel back to *Property Brothers* on HGTV. "Oh, I love this part. The reveal."

We watch the transformation for a few moments and comment on how much nicer the new house looks. When the episode comes to an end, Caroline puts the TV on mute and turns to face me.

"So...Tom has been arrested."

I'm so stunned, I nearly choke on my water

"My lawyer called and told me today. He pled not guilty, of course."

"So, what's going to happen now?"

"There's going to be a trial," she says. I lean a little closer to her to see whether her eyes are actually lit up or whether it's just the light from the screen streaming into the living room.

"You seem happy," I say, cautiously.

"I am," she nods. Her lips curl at the edges forming a delicate smile.

"Well, in that case, I'm excited for you."

"You're surprised," Caroline says.

I nod. Actually, she's right. I am more than surprised. I'm shocked. I've never been part of any situation like this, but I've read about other victims and witnesses and most of them are not that excited about the idea of going to trial. When I tell Caroline this, she just laughs.

"I'm actually kind of caught off guard by this as well," she admits. "All of these days I didn't know what I was feeling or how I was supposed to feel. And then my lawyer called and told me about the trial and it was like this big weight was lifted off my shoulders."

"And you're not afraid of what might happen at trial?" I ask before I get the chance to stop myself. I hate it when I speak before I think. I mean, why even bring this up if she's feeling so good right now?

But Caroline just laughs. "Of course, I don't know what's going to happen. But I'm sort of looking forward to testifying. The thing is Ellie, that I'm really angry. Mad. I feel it all the way down in the pit of my stomach. And telling the jury what he did to me so he can pay for it, well, actually, I can't wait."

"Oh my god, you are much braver than I am. You're kind of amazing, Caroline," I say and wrap my arms around her.

"You know, you're going to have to testify too," she adds. My heart sinks to the bottom of my stomach and my fingers turn ice-cold. But I force a smile.

"Of course, I will," I say quickly. "That asshole needs to go to jail for what he did."

Before we get a chance to talk about this anymore, the buzzer rings. Someone's at the front door.

"Who is it?" I ask into the intercom.

"It's me," Aiden says. A big wide natural smile comes over my face as I buzz him in.

CHAPTER 29 - AIDEN

WHEN HE SHOWS UP…

*M*y heart skips a beat and the end of my fingertips get that familiar tingly feeling.

"What are you doing here?" I ask, opening the door. Aiden smiles and shrugs his shoulders. A few strands of hair fall into his face, making his eyes even more mesmerizing. He leans on the doorway and runs his tongue over his luscious lips.

"I should've never left," he says slowly. "I'm sorry."

I nod.

I'm about to invite him in when he takes my hand in

his and pulls me toward him. Aiden wraps his arms around me and suddenly all my worries melt away.

I know that no matter what, we're going to be okay. Everything is going to work out.

Slowly, he runs his fingers up my spine, eventually settling at the nape of my neck.

I let my head drop into his hand. Holding me up, he presses his lips onto mine.

It's a slow, passionate kiss that seems to last forever. It's one of those kisses, which you remember for a lifetime.

When I'm ninety and I find myself sitting on my front porch with my granddaughter and she asks me what it means to be in love, my mind will immediately go to this kiss.

"I'm sorry," he whispers again as he pulls away.

"No, I'm the one who should be sorry. You had such a hard day and you still went to dinner with my folks. But why did you? We could've rescheduled."

"Eh, I don't know. I promised you that I would. But I

should've told you about getting fired sooner. I was just...embarrassed."

I give him a warm hug. I can see that admitting this fact made Aiden grow weak at the knees.

"So, why did you come back?" I ask.

"I don't know. I made it a few blocks before it hit me. We both had really shitty days, so why the hell should we be apart? I mean, I thought I wanted to be alone, but that's just because that's what I'm used to doing when I have a bad day. But the further I got away from your house, the more I realized just how much I missed you."

"I'm glad you're back," I say. "I didn't want to be alone either."

I stand on my tiptoes and kiss him. I bury my fingers in his thick hair and pull slightly until he gives out a moan.

"Caroline is in the living room," I say, pulling away. The warning is not really necessary since he's going to find this out momentarily anyway.

We walk to the living room holding hands.

"Hey, how are you?" Aiden asks.

"Oh hey," Caroline says, turning around on the couch. "I'm okay, I guess. Better."

"Glad to hear that."

Caroline flashes him a small smile. We sit in the living room with her a bit. I want to take Aiden back to my room, but since she's out here, we both feel like we should spend time with her. Caroline flips through the channels and then settles on a re-run of *The Notebook*.

"Oh my god, what a cheesy movie," Aiden says, helping himself to a spring roll.

Caroline's eyes grow wide and she looks from him to me and then back again.

"What?" he asks.

"I don't know if you know, but this is your girlfriend's favorite movie," she says, bursting into laughter.

"It is not my favorite," I say quickly. I don't know why I feel the need to apologize or explain except that I know that it's sappy and romantic. And that's why I love it.

"Okay, *one* of her favorites," Caroline concedes.

"Okay, I'll give you that," I say.

"Seriously?" Aiden asks.

I nod and shrug.

"Is it all because of Ryan Gosling?"

"Well, yes, and no. I mean, I just love him and Rachel McAdams together. And this movie...it's perfect."

Aiden laughs. "I have no idea how we made it this far into our relationship without this coming up. But now that I know...I don't know if I can keep this thing going."

"Oh please," I wave my left hand at him. Aiden grabs it and pulls me close to him.

"Oh my God, please. You two are so cute and in love, you're making me gag," Caroline says. "Don't you know that I just got out of the hospital?"

"Okay, okay, I'm sorry. That was my fault," Aiden says and pushes me away from him. "Oh hey, wait a second. Where's your ring?"

He looks at my hand and then up at me. I shrug.

"I took it off because we were going to my parents' house. And I didn't want them to know until it was the right time."

"Wait a second," Caroline sits straight up. "Ring? What ring?"

Aiden and I exchange looks.

"What ring?!" Caroline demands to know. Finally, I smile and cave.

"Aiden...asked me to marry him," I say.

"He did? You did? And what did you say?"

I walk over to my purse, fish out the ring from the inside pocket and put it on my finger. Then I walk over to the couch, holding my left hand in the air, to showcase the ring.

"Oh my God! Oh my God!" Caroline squeals and runs over to me. "Ellie! Oh my God!"

She keeps going back and forth between hugging and kissing me and admiring my ring. From her reaction, you'd think that she was the one who got engaged. I glance over at Aiden and he's equally surprised.

"Wow, I had no idea you would be so happy," I say. "I mean, I knew that you would be happy for me...but still."

"Of course! This is the most exciting thing that's happened...in a very long time. And this ring...you did good, Aiden. Really good," she says. "Oh Ellie, you have to let me help you plan your wedding."

I inhale deeply. Plan my wedding. Wow. Of course, this is the natural next step after a person gets engaged, but somehow the idea of actually having a wedding didn't occur to me. My heart skips a beat. I'm not a huge fan of parties and the thought of having one where I would be the center of attention makes me sick to my stomach.

"I'm sure you already know what kind of dress and venue you want, but I really want to be there when you make all the arrangements," Caroline gushes.

And that's where she's wrong. I actually have no idea what I want. To tell you the truth, I have devoted exactly zero thoughts to this subject.

"Are you sure?" I ask.

"Yes, of course!" Caroline's eyes light up.

"Ellie, I think you have to let her do it," Aiden says. "I mean, look how happy she is."

Caroline grins from ear to ear. "But honestly, Ellie, in all seriousness. I'm really happy for you, both of you. And it would be just the biggest honor to help you plan even a few aspects of this momentous event."

This brings tears to my eyes. Before I completely break down, I wrap my arms around my friend and kiss her on her cheek.

"I'd love for you to help," I whisper into her ear.

"*I* still can't believe how excited Caroline is for us," I say.

"I know. I was really not expecting that either." Aiden makes himself comfortable on my bed as I wash my face and remove my makeup in the sink.

"I was actually worried about telling her. I mean, she went through so much in Maine and I didn't want to throw it in her face about how happy I am."

"Are you that happy that you are worried that you will make someone jealous?" Aiden jokes. I roll my eyes. "No, I know what you mean."

He gets off the bed and walks over to me.

He puts his arms around my waist and kisses my neck as I try to get soap out of my eyes.

It's still hard to believe that we haven't known each other for that long.

It feels like we have been together forever. And yet, every moment also feels like it's completely new.

"I love you," he whispers and licks my earlobe.

"I love you too, but you have to let me wash this stuff from my face. It's starting to sting."

He loosens his grip a bit, but doesn't let me go. My knees grow weak.

I feel myself melting into him.

He intertwines his fingers into my hair and pulls on it slightly.

I moan as my whole body tingles in pleasure.

He then moves my hair off my shoulders and kisses me forcefully.

I bury my hands in his hair, moving his head toward mine. I feel his cock swell and I can't help but grab it.

"No," he says, smiling.

"What? Why?"

"You ask a lot of questions, do you know that?"

"Yes," I smile. I don't know if he knows, but these coy conversations drive me wild.

Without saying another word, he pulls off my clothes one by one. I try to protest, but he simply puts his finger over my mouth.

"Shh," he whispers. I let him do as he pleases, watching the way the soft light wraps itself around us.

After running his hands over my thighs, Aiden positions me across his chest.

He pulls off my bra and frees my breasts.

I run my fingers up his arms, watching the veins bulge in and out with each movement.

I lose myself in the moment as he cups my breasts with his big warm hands.

His hands are strong. Even after all of this time, I'm surprised by just how powerful they are.

His suits are quite deceiving in this respect.

A moment later, I'm standing completely naked before him. Normally, I would feel vulnerable and exposed, but in his arms, I just feel loved.

His lips make their way down to my nipples as I thread my fingers into his hair.

Shivers run up my spine as he presses my nipple in between his teeth.

He sits me back down on his lap, facing away from him.

He walks his fingers down my body and my legs spread before him.

He easily finds my clit and, when he touches it, my whole body starts to throb for him.

My thighs clench, but I open them up again and inhale deeply.

Despite all of this time, I still have trouble receiving pleasure and letting a man just focus entirely on me. But when I let go, that's when I finally feel free.

Aiden kisses me behind my ears as his fingers get deeper and deeper within me. They start to move faster and faster and I feel a rush of warmth concentrate in between my legs. Suddenly, a surge of energy starts to build within me.

"I'm getting close," I warn.

"That's what I want to hear," Aiden says, and speeds up his movements.

"Come for me," he orders, and his fingers swirl faster and faster.

This command sends me completely over the edge. My whole body starts to shake and vibrate with pleasure. A few moments later, I collapse on top of him. The release is so intense that it made my mind go completely blank.

CHAPTER 31 - ELLIE

WHEN A BOMB DROPS...

*T*he following morning, I sit down to finish the third book in my series, *Auctioned Off*. I'm surprised by how well the writing is going. The words are just flowing out of me and I can barely keep up. I guess that's the thing about writing about your life. There isn't much to make up and there's plenty of material to rely upon. As I get to the chapter with another sex scene, I pause for a moment and stare at the cursor on my computer screen. Despite my best efforts to keep these kinds of thoughts at bay, my mind goes back to dinner last night and the hurtful things that my mom said.

The thing that she doesn't understand is that writing

about sex is very liberating. In our culture, sex is a very popular topic of conversation. It's something we often discuss on talk shows and in magazines. But these discussions are clinical and sterile. There are always evaluations of how much sex people are having, a rating of how good it is, or practical steps to making it better. The thing that isn't discussed very often, though, is pleasure.

When I write about sex, I want my readers to enter a world where sex isn't something that happens behind closed doors. I want them to enter a world where sex is a beautiful thing that's shared between two people who are in love. I want to transport them to a place where anything is possible. But it goes beyond my readers even. When I'm writing, I don't think about the people who will eventually read my books. No, I write for myself. And in the case of this series of books, I write to put down my own experiences.

Sometimes, I find it hard to believe that Aiden is real. I find it even harder to accept that we went through everything that we went through. So, writing it down, exactly as it happened is my way of processing it. I'm recording the truth, as I have experienced it. If Aiden were to write this story, I'm sure that it would be a little different than my own, but that's the thing about perspectives, isn't it? We each have our own and we each live in our own reality according to our perceptions of the world around us.

Before I start writing the first sex scene in the third book, I take a moment. I close my eyes and take a deep breath. I let it out slowly as I open my eyes. Now, when my fingers touch the keys of my laptop, I'm free to write what I want. My mother's opinions about my chosen profession and her attitude toward the things that I choose to write about in my books no longer matter. They get buried somewhere in the back of my mind, a place that I will not access for at least the rest of the afternoon. I don't know if this is what it's like for others who slice open their wrists and bleed in words, but that's what it's like for me.

An hour later, I finish the scene and crack my knuckles. My hands are cramped from typing so fast and I'm turned on from reliving one of the hottest nights that I've shared with Aiden. I'm pretty sure that everyone who will read this book will assume that it's all fiction, but it gives me great pleasure to know that it's actually 100% true. I could easily change the front matter and call it non-fiction, but I'm not sure I'd sell as many copies. Or perhaps, I would sell even more. Who knows?

Before I get up from behind the desk and take a proper break, I check my KDP dashboard. Wow, twenty books sold already today. My whole body rejoices. I don't know how many copies the top authors sell a day or how much money they make, all I know is that every sale makes my heart soar. I'm eternally grateful and thankful for the fact that there are people out there who are not only enjoying my work but also paying to read these books. Growing up, I always wanted to be a writer. I love the process of writing, it's one of the most cathartic things I've ever experienced. But the thing that surprised me most when I started publishing was how much I enjoyed the feedback that I get from my readers. Suddenly, writing no longer seems like such a solitary exercise. Instead, I gained an audience that really engages with me and my work.

* * *

After spending so much concentrated time hunched

over the computer keyboard, it feels good to stretch my limbs. I raise my hands above my head and do a couple of sun salutations. Just as I'm about to close the computer, I get a Google alert.

Hmm, what could this be?

When I first started working at BuzzPost, Caroline set up a Google alert for me to my name. It never would've occurred to me to do that but Caroline said that since I was now going to be a proper writer with a byline and everything, I need to be alerted whenever my name appears anywhere else on the web. I'm not sure if this really needs to be said, but I've never been alerted before for anything except for my own articles.

The first thought I have when I see my name is that BuzzPost must've re-published one of my old quizzes and that's why the alert came up all of the sudden. The alert is set up only with my real name - I have no idea why I thought that I should publish inane online quizzes using Ellie Rhodes instead of a pseudonym - so this definitely doesn't have anything to do with my romance books.

Oh my God.

My mouth drops open reading when the page loads. I can't believe it. No, this can't be happening.

Shit.

Shit.

Shit.

The article that appears on the screen is not just some online gossip rag that no one reads. Oh no. It's the fucking New York Post.

I'm on Page Six of the *fucking* New York Post.

I look at the pictures first. There's a picture of me from my Facebook profile. Then there's the picture of Aiden and I together from the Daily Dish. And then there's the cover of my book, *Auctioned Off*.

Shit.

Shit.

Shit.

I skim the article. Then I read it more thoroughly. Then I re-read the parts that are particularly damaging to make sure that I didn't misunderstand anything. No, it's pretty much as bad as I had thought. Unfortunately.

My heart sinks into the pit of my stomach and I stare at the window for a while, losing myself in a trance. What can I really do about this?

I lose track of time. When I finally come to, I notice that more than forty minutes have passed with me just sitting here staring into the abyss. The screen has gone dark, but when I press the power button, it all comes back. The first thing that I see is that stupid Page Six article. This story has exposed me not just as a romance writer, printing both my real name and my pseudonym, but also as the girlfriend of the recently fired CEO of Owl, Aiden Black. If these were the only things that the article mentioned, that would've been bad enough. But it's worse. Much worse.

In addition to all of that, the article also discusses the auction. According to some anonymous source, the writer mentions that Aiden and I first met when I allowed myself to be auctioned off for a large sum of money. Whoever talked to this writer was there. He or she didn't get the full amount exactly right, but they were only off by ten thousand dollars. Of course, we could deny all of this. I mean, it's so outrageous, who would believe it, right? Except that my fucking novel confirms pretty much every aspect of it.

I feel sick to my stomach. I don't even make it all the way to the bathroom before vomiting. When I do finally reach the toilet, it seems like everything I ate during the last two days comes up.

After I feel a tiny bit better, I wash my face and look at myself in the mirror. It's not a pretty sight to say the least. My eyes are puffy, my mascara is runny and my lips are swollen. *** And the worst part of this whole thing? As horrible as I look, I feel ten times worse.

My phone goes off. It's my mom. I press ignore. I'm not interested in anything that she has to say. She leaves a message and then texts me as well. When I don't reply, she continues to write as if I did.

· · ·

*C*ALL *ME.*

Where are you?

Have you seen Page Six today? There's an article about you and Aiden. And the auction. Is that where you met??

Call me as soon as you get this.

I SHAKE my head and toss my phone on the bed. I don't know how to deal with any of this. A few moments later, Caroline bursts into my room.

"Have you see Page Six??" she yells.

This is the most animated I've seen her since Maine. Well, except for when we told her about our engagement. Nothing like a little gossip and drama to get her out of her funk.

I nod and hang my head.

"Oh my God, what are you going to do?" she asks.

"I have no idea," I say, shrugging. "Everything just turned to shit."

"They mentioned the auction on the yacht."

"I know. That's the worst thing. And my book pretty much confirms their story."

Caroline sighs. "It's going to be okay. Maybe it will just blow over?"

"I sort of doubt it."

"What I mean is that maybe Aiden isn't that famous. And we both know you aren't."

"Thanks?" I say, not knowing exactly where she is headed with this whole thing.

"No, what I mean is that Aiden is important and all, but it's not like he's a celebrity. And neither are you. So maybe this story won't really matter to anyone."

"That would be true except for the auction bit. Wealthy men buying women on a yacht? Trust me, this story is going to stick around because it's going to sell papers."

"Papers?"

"You know what I mean. Generate clicks, whatever."

"Well, let's hope you didn't make it into the print edition," Caroline says.

I nod and exhale deeply.

The buzzer goes off. Caroline goes to see who it is.

"Who is it?" I ask when she comes back to my room.

"Aiden."

"You let him up?"

"Of course, I let him up. He's your fiancé."

She's right. Of course, she's right. Still, he's the last person I want to see right now. None of this is my fault and yet it is. At least, it feels like it is.

When Aiden appears in the doorway, Caroline says hello and then leaves us alone. I can tell by the look on his face that he already knows.

"I thought you were busy today," I say.

"I was."

I nod and wait for him to continue. I have no idea where to start so all I can do is let him take the lead.

"Have you seen Page Six?" he asks. I nod and look away.

He sits down on the bed next to me. "It's a fucking mess, Ellie."

"I know."

"I don't know what to do," he says, hanging his head. "My attorneys want me to deny the whole auction bit ever happened. It's a PR nightmare."

"I know."

"It's not really something that I can really explain without sounding like a total asshole," he says.

"So, what if you deny it? Can't you file a defamation or slander lawsuit?"

"I could if it weren't true," Aiden says. "The thing is that whoever is the source of this story, he or she knows a lot about what happened on that yacht. I mean, it happened pretty much the way they described it in the article."

I know all of this.

"I'm really sorry."

"This is such a cluster-fuck, Ellie. Maybe we could deny the whole thing but your novel pretty much confirms the whole thing."

"It's fiction," I whisper.

"Except that it's not. I mean, you say that it is, but we both know that it's not. And them outing you as a romance author and the writer of *Auctioned Off*, well that's as much corroboration as they need to make everyone believe that what they're saying is true."

I nod and stare at the floor.

"You know what?" I say. "So what?"

"So what?"

"Yeah, so what? We're all consenting adults. It's not like anyone was auctioning off women who weren't into it. It was just a game."

"Yes, but that's not really how it looks in the paper."

"You didn't do anything illegal, Aiden."

"Are you serious, Ellie? I paid you to have sex with me."

"It was a tip."

"I facilitated other people paying for, and getting paid for sex," Aiden says. "And even if this whole

thing blows over in terms of the police getting
involved, I'm never getting my job back at Owl now."

"What?"

"Yeah. Not a chance. CEO's have to be held to a
certain standard. No investors, let alone anyone on
the board of directors, will want to have me
anywhere near that company anymore. It makes
them look bad and that's not something they can
tolerate."

I shake my head.

"I'm sorry?" I say.

"Is that a question?"

I feel like he's picking a fight. Like he's egging me on.
And I can't do anything to stop it.

"I don't know why you're getting mad at me over
this," I say.

"Because you were the one who wrote the book!"
he says.

"You supported it when I first started writing. You
said, you believed in my writing."

"I did and I do. I mean, if you want to write, then write. But I had no idea that your self-published book under a pseudonym would make my whole life go up in flames."

I shake my head.

"What, you don't believe me?"

"No, I don't. Your life was already in flames, way before this. You already got fired. Your investors already pulled out. This story...it's nothing. It's going to blow over. No one's going to care."

"Fuck you, Ellie. Those investors pulled out because of Blake. I worked my whole life to make Owl what it is today and now just as it's about to become huge, I'm forced to sit on the sidelines and watch someone else take the credit for it. Do you know how that feels?"

"No, I don't. And I'm sorry that this is all happening. I know that it's all because of Blake. And I also told you that there was no reason to keep what he did quiet."

"Are you saying that I prevented you from going to the cops?" he asks, incensed.

Frankly, I have no idea. That whole night is a blur, a bad dream. I definitely didn't want to go the police. I mainly just wanted to forget that any of that ever happened. But now, I'm no longer so certain that this was the right decision. Maybe if I had filed charges, none of this would've happened. I thought that by covering up his assault, he would just go away. I had no idea that he would have the gall to go after Aiden. I had no idea that he would get his investors to pull out of Owl and eventually get Aiden fired. He was the one who was wrong and now I doubt that anyone would believe me about what happened that night.

"No, that's not what I'm saying. I just think that we handled this whole thing very badly."

Aiden nods and looks down at the floor.

"This is such a mess, Aiden. I'm really sorry. I had no idea that any of this would turn out this way."

"Me either," he says quietly.

I walk over and put my arm around him. He brushes it off, but I try again. This time, he lets me keep it there.

"We're going to get through this. I promise."

Neither of us says anything for a while.

"The thing is, Ellie, that I've been giving this whole thing some thought today."

"What do you mean?"

"Well, when I met you, I had a thriving business whose main competitor was Amazon. We were on an upswing and everyone wanted to get in on the action."

"Okay," I say slowly. I have no idea where he's going with this, but I don't like the tone of his voice.

"And then I met you. And things just started to go awry."

I shake my head. "That's really unfair, Aiden."

"Fair or not, that's what has been happening. I know that none of this is directly your fault, except for maybe writing a romance book detailing every aspect of the auction and our sex life and then not protecting your pseudonym enough."

"Aiden—" I start to say as tears well up in my eyes.

"I know that I encouraged it, so it's probably all my fault. But still, I can't help but notice all the stupid little coincidences that have occurred since we started dating. And then things got even worse when we got engaged."

"What are you saying Aiden?" I whisper.

"I don't know what I'm saying," he says, walking over to the window. I take a deep breath. He's just talking out of his ass. He doesn't mean any of this. He's just angry and doesn't have anyone else to take this out on.

I stand a few feet behind him and peer into the darkness outside. Maybe he's right. Maybe this is all my fault. I shouldn't have written that book. But how could I have known that anyone would read it at all? How could I have known that someone would make the connection between this little self-published book by someone with a pseudonym and the real me?

"I can't do this anymore, Ellie," Aiden says, still facing away from me.

"What?"

"I can't. I really can't."

My heart skips a beat. And then another. I forget to breathe and feel dizzy. I want him to take it back. I need him to take it back. But when he turns around to face me, I can see by the expression on his face that this is not likely.

"I'm not sure I can marry you, Ellie," Aiden says after a moment.

"You're not sure?" I whisper in a last ditch effort to make him clarify his words.

"I can't marry you."

CHAPTER 33 - AIDEN

I leave her apartment with tears in my eyes. I love Ellie. I want to marry her. But not right now. The world is spinning out of control and I can't have her in my orbit. I know that I was wrong to blame everything on her. None of this is her fault. Actually, it's probably all mine. But it just feels like my whole life is imploding and I'm not sure I want her to see the person that I will likely become at the other end.

The challenges we face define us. Isn't that what they always say? We proceed with our lives thinking that everything is fine and that we're basically good people, until something happens that really pushes the boundaries of this idea. Are we really as good as we thought we were? Are we as talented? Maybe we are just hacks? Maybe we have just been lying to ourselves this whole time.

I don't really know what I'm thinking, nothing makes sense anymore. All of my thoughts become like run-on sentences that melt together to form something foreign and strange. I climb into my car and press on the accelerator. Oh, how I wish that instead of being in the middle of Manhattan, I was somewhere out west where I could drive for miles down an empty stretch of highway without seeing another person. Maybe out there I could forget everything that has happened recently and find another way out.

But instead, I pull up to my building and give my car keys to the valet. I ride up the elevator and enter my empty apartment. The modern sleek design with sharp 90 degree edges and stainless steel appliances feels very far from home. This was always the place that gave me peace and comfort, and yet I feel none of that now. Now, it seems like something out of that old movie, Beetlejuice, and I would give anything to be in Ellie's small cramped room and in her arms again.

I know that I have done this to myself. If it weren't for me, Ellie and I would still be engaged. But despite the pain that I feel now, it felt like the right decision. Haste, yes. But also, not entirely wrong. Or maybe that's my mind playing tricks on me again?

After pouring myself a glass of cranberry juice and adding some sparkling water, I take a moment to enjoy the cold bubbly liquid as it runs down the back of my throat. It doesn't do much to make the feeling of complete loss go away, but it does focus my mind somewhat. Yes, Ellie wasn't too careful with her new identity as an author and perhaps I should've asked her not to write about the auction on the yacht in such precise and honest detail. But the story that appeared in Page Six didn't come from her. No, it had to come from someone who was there - and someone with an ax to grind.

The most obvious suspect is Blake. Of course. Why not, right? He attacked the love of my life, stole my company, got me fired as CEO and now he's going to embarrass me and make me look like a pervert in front of all of America. For someone who did the wrong thing, he sure does have an ax to grind. But why does he have all of this hatred toward me? For a long time, I thought that we were friends. I always considered him one of my closest confidantes. I had no idea that he had these deep-seated, dark feelings toward me. Was I just blind to it all? Or did I just ignore something that I should've spotted from miles away?

My phone goes off. It's Leslie Marks my public relations specialist. She's a woman in her fifties with four little kids. To say that she's a workaholic would be an understatement. And that's coming from a workaholic who surrounded himself with workaholics. No, Leslie is a cut above. She's either a chronic insomniac or she has made a deal with the devil to give her more hours in the day while the rest of us are stuck with only twenty-four. I used to have a whole team of PR people at Owl, but they never focused exclusively on me or performing any type of extensive damage control. Leslie, on the other hand, came recommended directly from my team of attorneys.

"I have a plan going forward," Leslie says as soon as I answer. She begins all conversations in the middle and I spend half the time playing catch up. I'm not sure if she does this because she's just a fast talker naturally or to save time.

"We need to go on the offensive. We need to find out who was the source of that article and discredit him."

Him. She means Blake except that she doesn't really know it yet. Neither do I, not for sure anyway.

"How do you know it's a him?" I ask.

"I guess it could be a her. Do you have any possible candidates?"

I do, but I'm not ready to disclose Blake's name yet. The article mentioned the auction, and Ellie laid out a lot of details about the process in her book. But there was no mention of Blake in either story. Not even a hint. And no matter how much I hate him, I have to tread carefully. There's Ellie to consider.

"I have a really good private detective. He will get to the bottom of this, one way or the other."

"And if he is able to find out who the source is," I say. "What then?"

"Well, once we know for sure, we go after him. Hard. Of course, that most certainly means getting your fiancée, Ellie, involved."

Shit. I haven't told her that I broke our engagement yet. I inhale deeply.

"Well, actually, things are sort of complicated with Ellie."

"What happened? You didn't break up with her, did you?" Leslie barks. Having been CEO for some time now, I haven't had the pleasure of anyone being quite so direct with me in a long time. It's actually somewhat refreshing. Being CEO, you exist in this bubble where everyone kisses your ass. And if you aren't careful, you might end up believing their lies that you do indeed walk on water. That's one of the most dangerous things that could happen.

"Aiden?" Leslie asks. "Are you there?"

"Yes."

"Listen, this is not a good time to have things complicated with Ellie. You need her on your side. She wrote that book. Who the hell knows what else she will do?"

"She won't do anything bad," I assure her. But she's way ahead of me.

"Actually, maybe you breaking up with her is actually a good thing. This way you can deny the whole auction thing all together."

I shake my head.

"Listen, let's talk about this later, okay?" I say, yawning.

"Okay, I'll call you first thing."

Last time she called me first thing in the morning, it was at five am. I tell her I don't want to talk her before nine and she begrudgingly agrees to wait until then.

When I hang up the phone, I consider Leslie's proposition. Perhaps I should tell her and her private investigator about Blake. He is the reason for all this shit. But I can't hurt him without hurting Ellie. When it first happened, she didn't go to the police and file a report. And to come out now would make it very easy for all those naysayers to not believe her. *Why didn't she come forward in the first place?* the better ones of them will likely say. And the cruel ones? Well, they will probably say that she deserved everything that happened because she let herself be auctioned off in the first place. No, all of those people can just go fuck themselves. I won't let them question Ellie's integrity. I won't let her go through that. Not for me. I love her too much.

CHAPTER 34 - ELLIE

WHEN NOTHING MAKES SENSE...

*A*fter Aiden left, every day melted into the next without much differentiation. Nothing seems to matter anymore. There is no reason to get up in the morning. There is no reason to go to bed. I stay up late watching television and I sleep at random times throughout the day. I can't manage to sleep more than two hours a time, but my body continues to crave some shut-eye so I start to exist in this perpetual state where I'm not fully awake nor fully asleep.

When I am awake, I cry. My eyes get puffy and stay swollen for days. No amount of ice, nor hot or cool teabags takes away the redness. It gets so depressing that after a while, I stop looking at myself in the mirror completely. Why does it matter what I look like? The sight of my uncombed and unwashed hair, a bathrobe that I've been living in for close to a week, if not more, and pale pasty skin is not something that I can face.

"Ellie, you have to snap out of it," Caroline says one day when the sun is shining brightly through my curtains. She comes in and opens them with one violent motion, making me squirm and hide my face under the blankets.

"You haven't showered or changed your clothes or been outside in days."

Okay, days is actually good. I thought it was longer.

"Many, many days," Caroline clarifies. Many, many days do add up to a week or more. This is less good.

"I can't today."

"You have to. This is the first sunny day we've had in a while and we have to go outside. You need to stretch your legs. Your muscles are probably all atrophied by now."

Caroline pulls my blankets off me and pulls me up by my arms. I want to protest, but that seems more work than to just go along with her. I let her push me into the bathroom.

"If you don't strip and get into the shower, I'll do it for you," she threatens.

"Can I have some privacy please?"

"No," she says. "But I will turn around."

I guess that's better than nothing. Slowly, I take off my bathrobe and pajamas and socks. My clothes definitely have a distinctively well-worn smell to them. Or is that just me? Perhaps, a shower isn't such a horrible idea after all. I turn on the water and wait for it to turn warm. When I see the steam rising to the top, I climb in slowly and let it cover me from my head to my toes.

"How does it feel?" Caroline asks. I close my eyes and lose myself in the pleasure. Every pore in my body seems to open up and welcome the refreshment. I lather up the shampoo in my hands and run it through my hair. The shampoo runs down my face and body and I revel in the feeling.

"Really good," I mumble.

"Told you."

After I get out of the shower, I wrap myself in a towel and flash Caroline a small smile. It's not much, but I'm making an effort. That seems to be enough for her.

"I'm tossing all of these clothes into the wash," she announces, probably half expecting me to protest. But I'm glad they're going. I've been wearing them since the night he told me he doesn't want to marry me and I can't stand the sight of them.

"How are you?" I ask. "I'm sorry I've been in such a funk and I haven't been here for you."

I'm a terrible friend, I know that. But there was literally nothing I could do.

"I'm fine actually. I guess all those days of moping around were good for me."

"And here you are trying to get me to stop."

"Wow, a joke?" Caroline says. "I guess you'll make it through this yet."

I roll my eyes.

"That's the thing about time, isn't it? It keeps going

even if you want it to stop. And as it marches on, it starts to take away some of the pain," Caroline adds.

I know she's right, but the idea of time healing all things is a foreign concept to me now. I mean, intellectually, of course, I agree. But deep down in my soul, my heart still hurts thinking about Aiden.

———

AN HOUR LATER, I'm doing something I didn't think I could ever do again, eat waffles for breakfast and enjoy them. Caroline makes them and slathers them in maple syrup. Oddly, they are one of the few things that she can make entirely from scratch.

"These are amazing," I mumble, as I stuff them into my mouth.

"Yes, they're pretty good, aren't they?"

We sit there in silence for a few moments enjoying the delicious breakfast. Just when I don't think I can stomach another bite, the buzzer goes off.

"Who could that be?" I ask, getting up. I wipe my mouth with the back of my hand before I press on

the intercom button. When I hear her voice, chills
run down my back.

"It's my mom!" I yell, running back to the kitchen.
Since I was the one who answered, I couldn't not let
her in. But now I'm freaking out.

"So what?" Caroline asks, clearly not understanding
the urgency of the situation.

I only have a few moments before she rides up the
elevator and walks over to our door. I glance around
the living room and the kitchen. There are things
around, but the place doesn't look that bad. I run
into my room. Now, this place is much more of a
disaster area.

"Can you get that?" I turn to Caroline when I hear
my mom knock on the door. The fact that I kept it
locked was not an accident.

While Caroline gets the door, I quickly cram all the
clothes and shoes that are coving my floor into the
closet. The closet door barely closes but with a little
bit of muscle and determination, I manage to get
it shut.

"Hey there," I say. When I give her a warm hug, I see

my reflection in the mirror on the wall.

Holy crap!

How could I forget?

Shit!

"Ellie, what's going on?" my mom asks. "You look...."

She doesn't finish her sentence because she hasn't seen me without makeup since high school. But today, the situation is much worse than me just not wearing a full fresh face. I'm freshly showered, but that doesn't exactly remove evidence of not sleeping and crying my eyes out for days.

"You look awful," Mom says, shaking her head.

"Gee thanks," I say.

"You know what I mean."

"I know, I'm sorry. I wasn't really feeling like myself for a while," I say, shrugging. I know that my mom doesn't really mean anything when she comments on my appearance, but that doesn't change the fact that it still hurts and makes me feel like crap. It's also the main reason that I always feel compelled to look perfect when I come over for dinner. Nothing can be off. Everything has to be perfect, otherwise she will make a comment about it and act 'concerned.'

"Mom, what are you doing here?"

"I had to come see you. I called and texted you a million times and I didn't hear back. I was getting worried."

"I'm fine," I say with a shrug.

"You don't look fine."

"She is, Margie," Caroline says. "She was just going through something."

"With Aiden?"

"Yes."

Mom shakes her head and crosses her arms at her chest. "That guy is trouble," she announces, as if she knows anything about him.

"I thought you would be excited about us being together. I mean, he is somewhat of a celebrity."

"Do you really think I'm that shallow?"

I shrug again. I didn't think so, but recently she has changed quite a lot. She has been hanging out with way too many people with apartments on Park Avenue and houses in the Hamptons. And with enough contact with them, things tend to change.

"Listen, you don't have to worry, okay," I say after a moment. "We're not together anymore."

"What?"

I take a deep breath. This part is so embarrassing. I mean, I just introduced him as my boyfriend and now it's over. Now, I know why people wait for months or even years to introduce their significant others to their parents. So, you don't have to go through stuff like this.

"Oh my God!" Mom gasps and grabs my left hand. As soon as I look down, I realize my mistake.

"What is this?"

"It's nothing," I say, and hide my hand behind my back. I had put my engagement ring back on last night when I was feeling particularly pitiful and sorry for myself and I had forgotten to take it off.

"This is an engagement ring!"

"Isn't it beautiful?" Caroline pipes in. If this is her

idea of a joke, it's not funny. I give her a look to shut her up.

"We're not engaged, okay? I forgot to take this off."

"But you were engaged. And you didn't tell me?"

"I was going to, but then things got kind of complicated at dinner."

Mom shakes her head and paces around the room.

"So, you were engaged when you came over? And you deliberately didn't wear the ring?"

"Yes, okay? So, what?"

"So, what? I thought that we were close, Ellie. I thought that we had a good mother-daughter bond and then you go and get engaged and don't even tell me. What the hell?"

I shrug. I don't really have an answer except that I have no idea what mother-daughter bond she's talking about. Ever since I became a teenager, we have always had somewhat of a cool relationship. We used to fight a lot, and now that we don't, we don't talk much anymore either. She hardly knows anything about me or my life and what she does know, she criticizes. This makes it kind of difficult to share new and potentially dramatic information about my life. Of course, I can't really go into any of this right now because it will just open a big can of worms that I'm not really equipped to deal with at the moment.

"Listen, I'm sorry I didn't say anything earlier. The conversation at dinner sort of went off the rails and it didn't seem like the right time. And now...well, it kind of doesn't matter anymore since we broke up."

"Was it because of what you wrote in your novel?" Mom asks. She's well aware of the Page Six article and, knowing her, she probably went out and researched me as a romance writer as well. I didn't explicitly tell her not to read my books, but I did warn her that they have rather sexually explicit content that she might not want to read (mainly, because the writer is her daughter). Initially, I was pretty certain that she hadn't read my work. But now with everything that has come out about it? I'm not so sure anymore.

"No, not really. He was really supportive of my writing actually," I say. It's hard to explain why exactly we broke up. I hardly understand it myself.

CHAPTER 35 - ELLIE

*M*y mom stays for the rest of the morning and into the afternoon, but luckily we don't spend all of our time talking about what a fuck up I am.

Instead, we actually manage to have an okay time. She asks me a bit about Aiden, but when I give her a few one sentence answers and don't elaborate, she lets it go.

Same goes for my romance writing career.

I still have no idea if she has read my books.

She doesn't mention them and I don't bring them up either.

When my mom finally leaves, I promise to call and text back whenever she contacts me. In return, she promises not to be so hard on my choice of career.

"I like your mom," Caroline announces after we both say goodbye.

"That's 'cause you didn't have to live with her for eighteen years," I say.

"Eh, she's not that bad."

"No, she's not," I concede. "We're just really different."

"Yeah, I can see that."

After a day of socializing, I'm exhausted. I head to my room for some much needed *me* time.

Hanging out with my mom tires me out on my good days, let alone when I don't have any time to prepare for her visit at all.

The truth is that I'm basically an introvert, so spending a lot of time with people can be quite exhausting for me.

I feel the need to perform and be on my best behavior - act friendly and sweet and kind when those are often the last things in the world that I want to be.

"Hey, so, I was thinking," Caroline pops into my room just as I put my favorite Christmas music playlist on Spotify on my phone.

"Yeah?" I ask, without taking out my earplugs. I don't want to do anything to encourage her to stick around longer than she absolutely must.

"What if we go out tonight?"

"Where?" I look out the window. It's already dark. Even though it's warm in our apartment, I can almost feel the cold wind blowing outside.

"I don't know," she shrugs. "Somewhere. A club maybe."

I shrug.

"Oh c'mon, please. I haven't been out in ages. And neither have you. I don't want to go out myself."

"I don't know," I say. "It's cold out there. I don't really want to put on high heels and a short dress."

"C'mon, you're going to look amazing. And when

you get hot guys hitting on you...well, that will be pretty awesome too."

"I don't need hot guys to hit on me to feel good."

"You may not need it, but it will definitely help," Caroline says. "Okay, fine. Just come dancing then. It will be good for both of us to get out given what we've been through recently."

She's right, of course. I know that. I've been spending way too much time hanging out in bed and on the couch, doing absolutely nothing.

"But why do we have to go out to a club? Why can't we just go out to lunch tomorrow when it's light out?"

"Because lunch isn't the same thing as going dancing. It's not as fun. It doesn't get your endorphins going the same way."

I continue to protest for a while longer, but eventually I give in. I think I give in because I know deep down that Caroline is right, but I mostly give in because everyone eventually does when Caroline asks them for something.

A FEW HOURS LATER, I am doing the unthinkable. I'm actually getting dressed to go out to a club.

I put on one of my most comfortable yet still club-appropriate dresses in my closet and a pair of black high heel boots.

Since the weather outside is below freezing, I also opt for a pair of tights.

This won't keep me that warm, but I know that I will be warmer than Caroline who is dressed in a short strapless dress, open-toe shoes and a light summer jacket. There's no scarf or hat in sight.

"You're going to get pneumonia going out like that," I say.

"Hey, go big or go home," she says with a smile. "Besides, we're just going to go in and out of a cab.

"And what if we have to wait outside in a line?"

"I'll deal with it."

Half an hour later, I find myself in the warmth of a

hopping club, where sweat quickly starts to roll down the small of my back.

I immediately regret the tights, and the closed-toe boots, but there isn't much to do about it. Luckily, they have a coat check.

After Caroline and I get our drinks at the bar, we start dancing.

I brace myself for the headache that I'm sure is about to come on at any moment now.

I've never had a migraine, but I am prone to annoying pain at the back of my head especially when I find myself in hot, crowded places.

But as we start dancing, something unlikely happens. The tension in my shoulders quickly starts to vanish. One song replaces another and we start to dance harder.

I no longer care that I'm drenched in sweat. I'm just enjoying moving my body to the beat and lose myself in the music.

I completely forget to worry about a possible headache and an hour later, when we take a little break to get another drink, I realize that I never got one.

As we wait for our drinks, my feet continue to move to the music. I hate to admit it, but coming dancing actually did improve my mood.

Somehow, it lifted all of my worries away and made me forget about all the things that I've been obsessing about for the last few days.

CHAPTER 36 - ELLIE

"*I*'m going to the bathroom," Caroline yells into my ear over the music. Still, I barely hear her.

"Do you want me to come with you?"

"No, I'm good."

I head back out to the dance floor and lose myself in the crowd. Most people are paired off into couples, grinding on each other as a prelude to what is to come later. But I feel totally content dancing by myself. There isn't much separation between me and everyone else so it's not like I'm all alone in front of the world. No, this feels good. More than good. Amazing. As my body moves to the beats blaring from the speakers, I lose myself in the expression. Words and thoughts melt into my physical experience and I'm able to show the crappiness that I've felt about the breakup through my movements.

I've taken dancing lessons when I was a little girl, but I'm not much of a dancer. Still, in this moment, it finally hits me why some people are so driven to dance. The exhilarating feeling seems to fill every crevice and molecule of my body. And for the first time since he called off the engagement, I feel like maybe I'm going to survive this after all.

I don't know how much time passes as I dance, but when I look down at my phone, I realize that it has been more than forty minutes since Caroline left.

I head straight there. Slowly, I make my way through the crowd, which only intensifies near the bathrooms.

"Hey, the line starts back there," a girl says when I almost get to the entrance.

"I'm just looking for a friend," I explain and walk past them toward the stalls.

"Caroline?"

The bathroom is actually quite spacious with more than twenty stalls. I can't imagine how long the line would be if it weren't this big.

"Caroline!" I yell when I spot her sitting at the far end of the waiting and makeup area, on the floor, behind the couches.

The couches are overflowing with women in gorgeous dresses laughing and talking amongst themselves, paying absolutely no attention to the tears streaming down Caroline's face.

"What's wrong?" I run over.

"I don't know," she mumbles through the tears. "I just started crying and I couldn't stop."

"Did something happen?" I ask and immediately regret it. Of course, something happened. It happened back in Maine and being here has just brought it all back up to the surface.

"I don't know," Caroline mumbles as I wipe her tears. "This guy came up and hit on me while I was in line. He was very sweet and ridiculously hot and I just couldn't deal with it. I wanted him to leave, but we were both in line and...I just felt trapped."

She chokes up when she says the last bit and my heart breaks for her.

"C'mon, let's get out of here," I say, helping her up.

"But you were having such a good time."

"No, I wasn't," I lie. "I was just pretending because I thought you were."

"Really?'

"Yes, of course. It's hard for me to be out here. I just don't think either of us are ready to party quite yet."

She smiles. "This is just dancing. I'm not sure it's much of a party."

"Okay, okay," I say, shaking my head. "I see that you're not that upset since you still have the energy to make fun of me."

"Oh, you know, I love you."

Caroline and I walk hand in hand to the coat check. I get her ticket and hold her up as we wait for other people ahead of us to get their coats. The fact that everything around here has a line makes it feel like Disneyland, but with no kids. I want to ask her more about how she's feeling while we wait, but it doesn't feel like the right time. Instead, we talk about what we're going to do when we get home. Neither of us are really sleepy, so we decide to rent a couple of stupid movies on Amazon and watch them.

"What kind of movie do you want to see?" she asks.

"I don't care. As long as it's stupid and mindless," I say. Caroline starts to go through possible options on her phone. I tune her out a bit and look around. There are happy couples all around. Some have known each other for some time. Others have just met and are just at the beginning of whatever their relationship is going to be. It might last only a few hours and they will never see each other again. It might last until morning, a few months, or a lifetime. That's the thing about meeting the love of your life, isn't it? You never know when and where it will happen.

And that's when I see him.

He walks past me and into the main dancing area of the club. The thing that makes my heart sink is not that he's here, but the fact that there's a gorgeous blonde with her arm around his shoulder. She gives him a peck on the cheek as they walk past us and whispers something funny into his ear.

"I have to go," I say to Caroline. My chest seizes up and I can't breathe.

"What? But you need to get your coat."

I manage to press both coat check tickets into her hand before everything turns to black. My feet carry me outside where the cold air hits me like a ton of bricks. I can't catch my breath and I feel like I'm going to pass out. I want to run, get away from this place as fast as possible, but my chest seizes up and all I can do is kneel down to the ground and wrap my arms around my knees.

"Ellie?" Aiden asks. "Are you okay?"

CHAPTER 37 - AIDEN

WHEN I SEE A LIGHT AT THE END OF THE TUNNEL...

I never knew that it would be so difficult to be unemployed. I've never not worked before. Even though I seemed like a slacker growing up, not paying much attention in school and turning in many homework assignments late, I spent all of my free time working on computers. And once I started Owl, that's pretty much all I've been doing. The idea of working for forty hours a week was pretty foreign. I typically put in at least sixty hours. But the thing about doing something you love is that it doesn't really feel like work. Sometimes it does, you get tired and need a break. But most of the time, the work itself fuels the sleepless nights. If I couldn't sleep, I would just get up and work through it.

And now? Well, now things are different. I'm not allowed to set foot in my company. I stopped contacting people who I considered my closest friends because most wouldn't respond to my emails and calls. In a matter of a few weeks, my whole life has been hijacked. Taken. Kidnapped. All I'm left with is a huge severance package and a signed non-disclosure agreement promising never to talk about any of this again.

Poor me, right? God, all of this makes me sick to my stomach. I'm actually complaining when there are lots of people out there who get fired without so much as a good-bye. They aren't given millions of dollars of their company's money to just go away. When they are told to get the hell out at Christmas, they get to go home wondering how the hell they're going to afford their kids presents that year and pay rent. Or their health care insurance payment.

I know that I'm incredibly lucky, but I still can't help but feel like shit. I walk around my apartment and suddenly hate the cold, modern way in which it's decorated. When I first hired the woman who did it for me, I loved this look. Contemporary and rich. Everything is a tone of silver, white and grey. But now the place just reminds me of a hospital. And not even a hospital, the morgue. The sterility of this place makes me sick to my stomach.

I'm lost. I'm not ashamed to admit it. I have no idea what I'm supposed to do with myself now. Owl was my life for all of my adult life. How am I supposed to just pick myself up and start something else? I guess I could get a job. But who the hell is going to hire a washed up CEO who got fired from one of the biggest start ups around? Besides, I'm pretty unqualified for basically every position out there. And that's not even mentioning the fact that I don't really need the money.

No, the only way forward with any of this is to start something else. But the thought of that is too daunting to consider. I'm still mourning what I had lost, or what was taken from me. And I don't mean just Owl.

I try to focus all of my thinking on the company because thinking about her is just too painful. I made a horrible, irreversible mistake for which I know that she will never forgive me for. I hardly forgive myself for it. Breaking off my engagement with Ellie was the stupidest thing I've ever done. I want her back more than anything. I should've told her how I was feeling. I should've opened up to her about everything that I've been going through. But instead, I acted like a coward. I pushed her away. And now it's too late. She has probably moved on, or she will very soon. She's gorgeous and kind and when she walks into a room, she lights it up. Frankly, she deserves a lot more than me. She deserves someone outgoing and patient and loving. Someone who will treat her like the queen that she is, rather than cause her pain. She deserves someone who isn't a fuck up, someone who has their life together. I mean, what can I really offer her besides money? My eternal devotion and love, yes. But is that enough to get past all the shit that I come with as well? I don't know.

My buzzer rings. It's John and Annie and I let them up. They storm into my apartment like a hurricane, carrying bags of takeout and sweet gifts. I can't resist grabbing a cupcake from my favorite place down in Chelsea and stuffing it in my mouth. John is one of the Vice-Presidents from Owl, a guy I've known since I first hired him straight out of Massachusetts Institute of Technology. Annie is his fiancée. They've been together since high school. They are one of those couples that have never broken up once and have been eternally and blissfully happy since they first met. Annie's parents went through a bad divorce so the fact that they are only recently engaged is all of her doing. John has told me that if she had let him, he would've married her after their senior prom.

John and Annie are here to make me feel better. John complains about work and how busy things are at Owl and the bad direction that they're taking under the new CEO. I appreciate his efforts, but I doubt things are really that bad. Annie dances around the topic of Ellie without coming straight out and asking about her. When she finally does ask how I'm dealing with the breakup, I can't help but lie. Even though they're my close friends, how can I just come out and say that life isn't worth living without her?

"I have an idea!" Annie announces after we are all sufficiently stuffed with Chinese takeout. "Why don't we all go out dancing tonight?"

John starts to protest immediately, to say that he has two left feet would be an understatement. But Annie insists. It's up to me to break the tie. I'm about to say no, when for some reason I agree.

"Yeah, sure, why not?" I say with a shrug. I don't really know what has come over me, except that the idea of staying home and staring at the television screen for another night is not something that I can handle.

"What? Really?" John asks.

I shrug.

***

A few hours later, when they pick me up in the cab, we are all dressed to impress. John is still in shock over my agreement to go.

"You've been in such a funk lately," he says. "What made you change your mind?"

"I don't know. Just reached that point, I guess. Like that line from *Shawshank Redemption* - Get busy living or get busy dying, right?"

We arrive at the club that Annie has picked out a few minutes later. Though there's a line of people waiting in the cold to get in, the bouncer recognizes me and waves us through. It doesn't hurt that Annie looks amazing. Her long blonde hair catches every ray of light, her strapless gold dress and four-inch heels accentuate her curves. She puts her arm around my shoulder as we walk in and whispers, "It's going to be okay, Aiden. Everything is going to work out."

I nod and give her a small smile. John is a very lucky man and not because Annie is so hot. She's thoughtful and sweet and loving. In this moment, I would give anything to switch lives with John just so I could have with Ellie what he has with Annie.

Suddenly, someone runs into me. I get spun around and turn back toward the entrance. That's when I see the glimpse of her. I can't be sure it's her, but I have to find out.

"I'll be right back," I mumble and take off after the girl running from the coat check line.

This can't be her. What would she be doing here? No, I'm wrong and stupid for even thinking this. When I step outside into the freezing cold, I see a girl kneeling down on the pavement. Her head is buried in her arms.

CHAPTER 38 - ELLIE

"*E*llie?" Aiden asks. "Are you okay?"

I recognize his voice immediately, but it takes a moment or two gather my strength to look up at him.

"Ellie?" he touches my shoulder, sending shivers through my body.

"Hey," I say, getting up. He tries to help me, but I push him away. "What...what are you doing here?"

"Are you okay?"

"Yes, of course. Why wouldn't I be?" I say, wrapping my arms around my arms. Suddenly, I realize just how cold I really am. I can't feel my toes and

fingertips. I lick my lips and immediately regret it.
When a cold breeze comes through, they turn
to ice.

"I just saw you running out..." his voice drops off.

"I'm fine," I say quickly. Why won't you just go away?
I'm lying. He knows I'm lying. What's the point of
this stupid game?

Finally, Caroline comes out, carrying my coat.

"Aiden?" she asks, handing me my coat. I put it on as
fast as humanly possible, and relish in the warmth.
"What are you doing here?"

"I was just heading inside with some friends when I
saw Ellie run out."

Friends, huh? Okay, fine if that's what you want to
call her. I can't help but roll my eyes at his ridiculous
explanation.

I walk over to the curb and hail a cab. One pulls over
right away.

"Let's go Caroline," I say in my most decisive voice.

"Ellie, please, wait," Aiden grabs my arm. I turn to
look at him. A lump of tears is building up in the

back of my throat and I say a word out loud out of fear that they will all bubble to the surface.

The look on my face must say a lot because he drops my arm and Caroline and I get into the cab. As soon as we pull away from the curb, tears start to stream down my face.

Caroline takes my hand in hers and squeezes lightly.

"Oh my God, I'm so, so sorry," I mumble. "I'm supposed to be here for you and I'm acting like such a fool."

"No, it's fine. Really."

We don't talk much the rest of the drive and, when we get home, I immediately head to my room.

"Hey, are you going to be okay?" I ask. "I'm sorry that tonight didn't really work out."

"I'm sorry that I freaked out a little. It was just all too much, you know?"

I nod and we bid each other good-night.

As I change into my pajamas and climb into bed, my phone goes off. It's Aiden. I press ignore and put on some mindless YouTube video instead. A few moments later, my phone goes off again. This time it's a text from Aiden. I want to ignore it, but I can't. Against my better judgement, I open it.

———

THANK you for reading Black Bounds! Can't wait to find out what happens next to Ellie and Aiden? **One-click Black CONTRACT now!**

They can take everything from me, but they can't take her.

Mr. Black is coming back. With a vengeance.

"**I need you to sign a contract.**"

"What kind of contract?"

"A contract that will make you mine."

This time she's going to do everything I say.

She's going to hate it and then she's going to beg for more.

This is the game we play. It's our game.

But what happens when others find out? Will we lose everything?

One-click <u>BLACK CONTRACT</u> Now!

———

SIGN up for my **newsletter** to find out when I have new books!

You can also join my Facebook group, **Charlotte Byrd's Steamy Reads**, for exclusive giveaways and sneak peaks of future books.

I appreciate you sharing my books and telling your friends about them. Reviews help readers find my books! Please leave a review on your favorite site.

BOOKS BY CHARLOTTE BYRD

ebt series (can be read in any order)

DEBT

OFFER

UNKNOWN

WEALTH

ABOUT CHARLOTTE BYRD

Charlotte Byrd is the bestselling author of many contemporary romance novels. She lives in Southern California with her husband, son, and a crazy toy Australian Shepherd. She loves books, hot weather and crystal blue waters.

Write her here:

charlotte@charlotte-byrd.com

Check out her books here:

www.charlotte-byrd.com

Connect with her here:

www.facebook.com/charlottebyrdbooks

Instagram: @charlottebyrdbooks

Twitter: @ByrdAuthor

Facebook Group: Charlotte Byrd's Steamy Reads

Newsletter

COPYRIGHT

Made in the USA
Lexington, KY
01 September 2019